ELAINE
OF
CORBENIC

Tima Z. Newman

Savant Books and Publications
Honolulu, HI, USA
2015

Published in the USA by Savant Books and Publications
2630 Kapiolani Blvd #1601
Honolulu, HI 96826
http://www.savantbooksandpublications.com

Printed in the USA

Edited by Daniel S. Janik
Cover Art and Design by Dennis Krull

13-digit ISBN: 9780991562220

To Gabriel
and to Dennis who sent him the Launcelot card,
and to Sloggy who introduced me to Rilke
on a stairwell landing

ACKNOWLEDGEMENTS

With gratitude to all those who loved the story—especially Jo Ann Brown, Catherine Preus, Judith Serein, Mary Webb, Ericka Lutz—and whose encouragement, editorial input, patience and support over these many long years was deeply sustaining. With deep gratitude to and loving memory of Alfred Medcalf (d. 10/24/13), a wounded fisher king of great heart. And with grateful appreciation for the invaluable support, patience and dedication of Laila Ansari, Ariel Adams, Sharon Reynolds, Barbara McEnerney, and my Savant editor Daniel Janik.

A rendering of the story
of Elaine of Corbenic and
Sir Launcelot du Lac
based on the account found
in Sir Thomas Malory's
Le Morte d'Arthur

Afore the time that Sir Galahad was gotten or born, a hermit came unto King Arthur's court upon Whitsunday, as the knights sat at the Round Table.

And when the hermit saw the Siege Perilous, he asked the king and all the knights why that seat alone was empty. Sir Arthur and all the knights answered: "There shall never none sit in that siege but one, for it is death for any man else to do so."

Then said the hermit: "Know you who that one is?"

"Nay," said Arthur and all the knights, "we know not who he is that shall sit therein."

"Truly," said the hermit, "for he that shall sit there is unborn and ungotten. And this same year he shall be gotten that shall sit in that Siege Perilous, and he shall win the holy grail." Having said these words, the hermit departed from King Arthur's court.

After the feast, Sir Launcelot rode off in search of adventure, till on a time by chance he came to Pointe Corbyne...

—*Le Morte d'Arthur* by Sir Thomas Malory

PROLOGUE

Corbenic's valley lay hidden, in a corner of Lystenoys close by the sea, and it was not wholly by chance that any man found his way there, including Launcelot.

It was spring when he came; the hills of the valley were verdant, and the evening mists fragrant. Spring was short in that part of the country, except in the valley where the castle lay, where the mists rolled in from the sea, and a stream from the hill flowed into the river which bordered the castle's south wall. The rains were meager and often did not come, so that the land surrounding the valley was barren and wasted, the tufts of grass dry and sparse over the rocky soil. What green did come from the winter snow quickly browned and withered in the summer sun. That week though, in the rocky barren seacoast land of Lystenoys, spring was in the air, the sky was blue and the gorse blooming yellow.

She was not looking for love that day. It is true she had not passed through her youth without hearing minstrels' songs and dreaming girls' dreams of some noble prince bearing her away in marriage, away from her father's wasted land, away from her beloved, burdensome solitude. Or without images of herself embroidering tapestries in the solar room, young sons and daughters about her, and from the window seeing her lord arrive home from a long absence, dismount, enter the keep, and come to her.

Domesticity. Though Lady Breusen, under whose kindly tutelage she had been since birth, would have been surprised at such a desire, for she slipped away from her household tasks whenever she could. Ordinariness. Simple common days, with nothing more weighty than the daily mass in a dawn sunlit chapel, and the overseeing of a busy household: the spinning and weaving and sewing of her ladies, the tutoring of the pages, the distilling of scents and the making of salves.

Elaine of Corbenic had not passed through her youth, shared in the whisperings and laughter of her ladies, without at least some such images settling within the recesses of her dreams. And in some part, expecting that life, as did others for her. Though her father lacked wealth, and his land was no great lure, her blood was royal, and her face fair. There was, true, a strangeness about her family, the strain of mystery that hung about their lineage. Lystenoys lay sequestered far from the main thoroughfares of Britain, and Corbenic's valley was hidden. However, that the strangers were few who came through was of little import, for there were worthy enough lords in the court of Corbenic itself.

Yet in the end, she had no thought for the knights of her father's court. The aura of the grail that haunted her dreams was fullness enough for her. She was Elaine, daughter of the fisher king and of the lineage of the grail keepers, and the mystery of the grail, the sacred cup that lay within Corbenic's walls, was in her very blood. Nothing else could find space in her heart. Until Launcelot came.

ELAINE OF CORBENIC

CHAPTER 1

Her earliest memory of the grail was enshrouded in the echoes of timelessness: A shaft of sunlight through the single arched window unto the simple stone altar in the bare tower room's center, upon it a gold vessel. A stillness, shimmering of sunlight, penetrating her very core. And she, entering into the heart of the stillness, ever deeper, as if the vessel before her eyes drew her like a lodestone, drew her into the heart of space and of time.

"An ancient holy relic of which our family has long been the keeper," King Pelles had said summarily when she had asked him of it. "There is a saying," he began but then seemed to think better of it, and said only, "It is said to be the cup from which our Lord drank the night before his death...and the cup which caught the blood spilled from his lanced side..."

The king removed his gloves, handed them to his page, for he had just ridden in from hawking. Stalwart and solid in build, his beard streaked with grey, he regarded his young dark-haired daughter thoughtfully. "There was a custom in my father's time," he continued, "of bearing forth the grail at great feasts. It was my sister, your aunt, who had the charge and role, for it was borne in great honor. The tradition was that it be the fairest and purest maiden of the valley who should be its bearer."

"My aunt, my lord?"

"Philomena, the one who is now Abbess."

"Why did she enter an abbey, sire, when this holy cup was in her very keeping?"

"Perhaps she knew it lay to another to bear the grail to its destiny. She entered at the time of Pellehan's wound."

"Who then is its bearer now, my lord?"

The king had smiled at the earnest child before him. "You, child. You are the bearer."

CHAPTER 2

Pelles' words had haunted her thoughts. As the sea upon the sand, the words traced themselves within her soul. The numinous vessel called her. When she could escape her lessons and embroidery, she would slip away to the tower room to sit, quiet, before the grail. It drew her to itself, into itself, a golden vortex of stillness.

She spoke of it once to Pellehan, the fisher who was the king's brother, himself king until he had received his wound. She did not know the story clearly, only that one day in the castle he had been struck in the thigh by a knight named Balin and the wound had left him maimed ever since. Though the residual pain had etched his aging face with fine lines, there was a calmness in his manner that was ever reassuring to the young girl.

"Have you heard tell of the grail, old one?" she

asked, as she sat beside him on the grass in the shade of the willows by the stream.

He was mending a net, and only nodded.

"Is it true it is a sacred cup?"

He looked up at her, smiled indecipherably, bent back down.

"I do not know if Pelles truly believes it."

"Pelles? He does not and yet he does. He is not one for ceremony or ritual. That is why the processions at feast days have lapsed. Yet he is now Keeper of the Grail. I would not have left him its keeping did I not know he would fulfill its care well."

A silence fell. She watched the lapping of the water. "He said something else," she said. "About a saying. What did he mean?"

Pellehan was slow to answer, as if declining to speak. His eyes, indiscernible and deep as the river yet dancing with the sparkle also of its reflected light, regarded her.

"It is said that there is a mystery and a power in the grail through which wholeness can be found. That in being touched to the grail, the wounds that have maimed us will find healing. And where there was burnt land, trees shall grow, and streams flow," he said at last. "Some day the question will be asked, the secret touched…"

"Healing for you, old one?"

"Yes. And the lands that are wasted will be wasted no more and there will be healing for the desolate. If Britain be ready, the grace and power of the grail will be brought from this hidden corner of Lystenoys to all the great Isle; and if not, it will return to the hidden place from which it came, to be again sought, and refound."

"Old one, I will ask the grail the question. I will find its secret."

"It is no easy quest. It is said it can be found only by one with a purity of heart that seeks not to possess the grail but to ask its meaning, what it serves—and who is open to receive the question the grail asks of all who behold it. Only one whose life is poured into it to the full will find its meaning."

"I will be that one," she asserted again. "I will find it, if not today, then tomorrow."

"You speak truly: if not today, then tomorrow. If not during your life, during the life which follows."

"…the life which follows?" Her voice revealed dismay.

"Ah child, what do you know of time? There is the preparing of the ground, there is the sowing of the seed, there is the pruning of the vine, there are the rains and the snows and the generations which pass."

CHAPTER 3

In the years that followed, the golden cup in the tower room imprinted its mark ever more deeply in Elaine's heart as she sat silent before it, listening, as if to hear its secret. She sometimes brought there treasures she had found in her play, special pebbles from the stream where she swam. And it was to the grail also she brought the sharing of her own secrets, all her child's secrets that could not be shared with the mother she did not have, and the father who was often so distant. When there was sadness in her heart, great aloneness, or special joy, it was there she would take herself.

It was not only in the tower room, but shimmering through all of her days that the grail claimed her.

It was there in a moment of sun, streaking through storm violet on the windswept hills. In the utter quiet of dawn rising over the sea. In the trace of a falling star in the starlit immensity of the night, stillness all about.

And in other moments as when the bowl of wine was lifted during morning mass and for one short second the world stopped, and the surface of things opened and depth plunged into ever expanding depth, weightless and soundless like a feather falling in a dream.

Or once when, at the festivities to celebrate a cousin's marriage, all the children pressing forward to throw flowers upon the bride, and Bromwell, still a squire then, had touched her hand and said to her, "Soon when I am a knight I shall win your hand and you will come and be my lady." Something within her had raised its voice and said, *No, is that all: it cannot be all. To weave, to sit in the solar, tapestry before her, wife to her lord, all?*

A hawk soared above them in the sky, and her breath arced to its flight. *No, it cannot be all.*

"Elaine! It is the hour for sewing!" Lady Breusen would call to her. Down-to-earth, grey-haired Lady Breusen, ever struggling valiantly to impart a noble upbringing to her royal charge. And always it seemed, Elaine had slipped away.

In her twelfth year, Pelles restored the custom of the procession of the grail, saying simply, "For you are of age now." He told her one summer evening, after he had spent a long afternoon down by the river with Pellehan in his skiff, and henceforth, on the great feast days of the year, the young princess bore forth the grail from its place of solitude to the great hall.

What did it mean, she wondered still, to be bearer of the grail? The question threaded through her youth, like a butterfly through the waving grass.

So the years had passed, childhood giving way to maidenhood. Elaine listened to the minstrels' songs and dreamed, played along the woodland stream, and as she grew older, rode her horse along the headlands, watching the waves break into white foam.

She laughed with her maidens, pulled daisy petals with them, adorned her hair with flowers. Yet when Bromwell, long knighted and now a powerful lord in the king's court, noticed her developing beauty and renewed his attentions to her, she gave him little encouragement. She smiled sweetly at him, rode hawking at his side, played backgammon with him, lithe and graceful, but when he began to speak of love she turned her face away.

"It is the grail which woos her," laughed Heloise, one of her companions, to him. Fair and winsome, and of sunny disposition, had she not had her eyes set on another, *she* would not have been averse to the attentions of the courteous and patient lord, sturdy, broad-chested and portly.

"But your family holds the grail in their keeping," protested Bromwell to the princess. "You possess it now."

"The cup, yes, the gold form. But to penetrate its mystery, to find its secret, its meaning...?"

"For whom do you seek the grail's mystery, Elaine? For yourself? For Pellehan's healing? For Britain?"

"God knows. I do not. Does the swallow stop its flight to ask for whom or why?"

"It is said, you know it," Bromwell pointed out, "that the grail's power shall be discovered for the healing of the king and the land, and the grail brought to Britain —if it be ready—by the noblest and purest of the King Arthur's knights. You are noble and pure perhaps, but no knight. Is it not then for another to do? Rest your quest."

"Bromwell, I cannot."

"My lady..." he began, but she shook her head gently.

"There is a void within me, a deep fathomless hollow, chalice shaped, and it draws me, as a whirlpool draws its lover."

"Elaine, it is the spring of your womanhood calling you."

"My heart is not free to be given you," she whispered, in as near to a shout as a whisper can be, and she turned away.

ELAINE OF CORBENIC

CHAPTER 4

If it had not been for the dream and the fear that enveloped her in its wake, perhaps she would not have encountered Launcelot that spring day as she did. Perhaps he would have come and departed from her father's court, and she, untouched, given him no notice.

When she thought upon it in after years, there had been foretelling in the dream. In her waking, though, she had not remembered the prophecy that had provoked the curse intended to circumvent fate—but which proved only a milestone in its fulfillment.

In its way, the dream had been the beginning of the crossing of their paths.

There had been a traveling minstrel before the table that night, full of tales of the great King Arthur's court, and Elaine, who had heard Arthur's name before and the respect in the voices of those who talked of him, now heard the songs of his court at Caerleon-on-Usk, and heard of the deeds of those who until then had been to her only names: Gawain, Gareth, Bevedere, and Launcelot du Lac, son of the King of Benoic. The latter, the minstrel sang, held claim as the most fearless yet most courteous knight of Arthur's round table. Unmatched in arms, he was yearned for by the ladies of the court, held in honor by his peers, loved as a brother by the king.

"Launcelot's family entwines with ours," Pelles remarked offhandedly, "on both sides. His father is a descendent of Brons, the first grail king and brother-in-law to Joseph of Arimathea, from whom our own lineage traces."

"Aye, so I have heard said," the minstrel confirmed. "Also that whatever quest awaits the noblest of knights shall surely be his."

The king only nodded.

"And is he a bachelor still?" asked Heloise, never shy.

"Aye, but set no hopes, fair lady. He serves only the queen."

"Then alas."

The minstrel went on to describe the beauty of the ladies of the court.

"Tell us," Heloise asked, brushing back her long braid of flaxen hair, "is it true that King Arthur's sister possesses powers of magic?"

"Morgana le Fey? Aye, so they say. Dark powers. I could tell you more than one tale that has been told me. But you have your own fearsome wonders hereabouts, I have heard. What of the great dragon-serpent of Corbyne?"

"A superstition," scoffed Pelles, shaking his head.

"The townsfolk of Pointe Corbyne do not hold so, Sire," interjected Heloise, emboldened by her excitement. "They walk in terror of it, lest one day it emerge from the slab stone which holds it entombed."

"What would happen then?" asked Elaine.

"They say it would devour all the young maidens, beginning with the king's daughter," Heloise answered, looking pointedly toward Elaine.

"Enough! I'll not have the town's foolish talk set fears in my household," said Pelles firmly, casting her a silencing look.

"'Tis true," murmured Heloise beneath her breath as

she lifted a cup to her lips.

An inexplicable shiver passed over Elaine, as she shook a moth from her hair. She cast a glance toward Lady Breusen, who was known to have certain skills with herbs and potions, but the latter, concentrating on her mutton pie, seemed oblivious to the conversation.

Elaine drew her mantle closer about her. "Sing another tale of Arthur's knights," she bade the minstrel. And the minstrel, strumming his lute, began a song of the battle of Sessoine and of the fame won by Arthur and Launcelot fighting side by side. When he had finished, he went on to sing of the ambush of Burgogne and of how Launcelot with his ten thousand knights put to rout three score thousand.

The fire leaped in the hearth, casting long shadows against the walls, and the wind moaned through the hall. The king rose, and the court retired for the night.

Moonlight shone through the window arch as Elaine climbed into her bed. From where she lay she could see the full moon, a wing of cirrus clouds floating across its brightness.

Dreams floated across the surface of her sleep, fragments and images and darkness, a serpent in the midst of steaming vapor, and a witch seeking power. Then there appeared a minstrel playing his instrument in the moon's light and singing his tale, the words of which threaded through her sleep. And the words he sang were these:

When Morgana le Fey heard of a cup whose power was greater than all the spells she could ever hope to learn, she set out to find and possess it. And when she learned that it was not hers to have, and that the most beautiful maiden of the western realm was to bear to the noblest of Arthur's knights the son whose quest would achieve the grail, she grew wrathful.

She went to the western realm, found the princess, and bade her yield the grail.

"Lady," was the princess' response, "it is not mine to yield."

"Cling you to your cup, eh, fairest of maidens?" hissed the dark-hearted queen. "Heaven has not blessed me, who am surely of queens beautiful, knowledgeable and powerful enough, with this talisman it grants you. I cannot touch it—my magic finds its limits at its contour— but if you bear its honor, why my little one, you must also take on the weight of its horror.

"Let all the burden of fear be yours, for what is mysterious has its dark side, and let its dark side steam about you and suffocate you until, drowning in the darkness of fear, you forego of your own desire this tarnished cup to which you cling, and seek refuge in convent or queen's retinue. May you never mother this son who it's said will take the grail forever from my clutch. As a serpent may the coils of fear and darkness emerge from terror's tomb to devour you."

Elaine woke from the dream sweating and shivering. The walls about her seemed cold; the grey sky at the window, heavy and foreboding.

She awaited the mid-day dinner hour with eagerness. Surely at the king's side, all uneasiness would melt away like morning mist. Though she remembered little of the dream, what did remain in her memory was the serpent of Corbyne, and the dream's horror focused onto it. She would talk to Pelles of the buried serpent, and he would have it destroyed.

"My lord," she said to him when the company was seated in the hall, "the serpent of Corbyne, cannot you slay it?"

"Elaine, do not let foolishness haunt your thoughts,"

Pellas responded dismissively. "The serpent is only a superstition, a fool's tale. I choose to hear no more of the matter." And he turned his attention away, biting with gusto into a leg of mutton.

Pelles' words did not dissipate her fear; instead they left an odd disquiet with her. That he would not even hear of her fear, nor acknowledge the reality of its source, left her feeling even more threatened, alone in facing an unnameable danger. From that day fear walked with her, and what had once been old and familiar now became uncanny and weighty.

ELAINE OF CORBENIC

CHAPTER 5

A shadow began to lie over Elaine, crossing the sky and sun of her days. Not constant, but a sudden and frequent presence. One moment she would be riding through the woodland, rejoicing in the sunlight and its dappled patterns through the leaves. The next moment the darkness of the shadows would suffocate her breath.

Even by the sea, when she stood on the headland cliffs, watching the foam spray upward in the sunlight, suddenly the thunder of the waves would strike terror into her heart. And in the tower chamber of the grail, where once she had found only peace and wonder, now at times the shadows in the corners would impinge upon her breath, and sweat drench her forehead. That whole year the shadow lay over her heart. For the most part she kept it buried as well as she could; only now and then the fear emerged to suffocate her with its coils. The hours and the days that passed between, though, became marked with a new unsettledness, a new questioning.

She rode once from the valley at winter's end, away from the sea, out between the mountains that formed the valley's end, and along the craggy rocky barren slopes that encircled the valley.

The further she rode, the more barren and rocky became the landscape, the trees stunted, and the tufty grass brown. It had been so since the time of Pelles' wounding, they said, as if the land had responded in grieving outrage. The sky was empty and the sun without gentleness. It had been a dry winter, with little snow or rain. The brown barrenness of the wasteland moors seemed the counterpart of the serpent's tomb, as if it spread like a rust from the seaside town.

She looked back toward Corbenic. Corbenic, with her imperturbable father upon the throne, and in the river her maimed uncle fishing from his skiff.

Father or uncle, which? she silently wondered, remembering a story she had once heard, that the one had bequeathed his betrothed as well as his kingdom to his brother when maimed that ill-fated day. As if it mattered.

The robust king on the throne, who gave little credence to either the grail within his tower or the serpent below in the town, and had no help against the drought, did he hold any more power than the maimed fisher king?

Who shall deliver me from this wasted realm? Elaine thought, suddenly in despair. *One king maimed, the other oblivious. Who shall free me from the suffocation of this land's barrenness? And who shall free the land from the serpent's coils? Who shall release the grail's healing power?*

ELAINE OF CORBENIC

CHAPTER 6

The weight of her aloneness lay heavy upon Elaine, and the stark sun did not dispel her sense of dread. She turned her horse away from Corbenic's direction, and rode further out into the wasteland moors of the surrounding country.

Not too many hours distant she knew lay the convent of which her aunt was abbess, and, though she had never been in the vicinity, the thought to go there suddenly came upon her. What succor she might hope for there she did not know, but she felt bereft of any comfort from the very ones she had once turned to trustingly as a child, and there was no one in Corbenic's valley in whom she could confide.

The Abbey of the Holy Family was small, white-stoned, stark against the barren land. The low sun glowed upon the low white buildings as Elaine approached, and the bells were ringing from the belfry for vespers.

"My brother's daughter, welcome," the abbess said, receiving her in a small chamber at vespers' close, and greeting her with a kiss. "I will have word sent to Pelles of your safe arrival." Then she motioned her to a small table, where bread and honey and mead were laid out.

"Reverend Mother, fear hovers by me, suffocates me in its coils," Elaine said to King Pelles' sister. "Ever since a wandering minstrel's tale, I am haunted by dread, and by dreams of the serpent entombed in Corbyne's churchyard."

The nun looked at her kindly. "Corbenic lies not in the most sunlit corner of Britain. Nor, I fear, do your solitary wanderings bring solace to your spirit. You can ask your father to send you to the great Arthur's court at Caerleon-on-Usk where you can join the queen's retinue; the busy merriment will leave no time for the shadow of fear."

"But…"

"God is not sunlight on flowered slopes alone: He is also barren desert, night and terror. The grail sparkles in your dreams, I know, daughter of the fisher king, but, alas, did you not know also that the depths hold not only pearls but terrors, too? And that the pearls are formed from the womb of pain?

"It grows late, but not too late. Go back. Tell Pelles to send you to Caerleon."

Elaine shook her head. "If there is darkness, then I will walk through the darkness. I have no desire to go to Caerleon."

The abbess smiled gently. "Then go take your rest, my niece. We will speak again on the morrow."

As Elaine turned to leave, the abbess added, "The buried serpent of which you spoke, know you that faintly etched in the stone slab marking its tomb are the words: 'Here shall come a leopard of king's blood, and he shall slay this serpent, and this leopard shall engender a lion in this foreign country, the which lion shall pass all other knights'?"

"I knew it not."

"I dare say not: few would be those who dared approach close enough to decipher the words, so worn away by time over the generations."

"Words so worn by time give little solace," responded Elaine. "Yet what is the inscription's meaning

—a leopard of king's blood engendering a lion?"

"Some answers only time shall reveal," the abbess replied. "It is late now, and time for you to take rest, my child."

A gentle peace, and a strange longing, lay over Elaine, as she listened to the voices of the sisters during compline, and she slept the night soundly, waking only for the sounds of the bells.

After the morning mass, she walked with her aunt in the enclosed garden. The sun cradled the flowers in warmth and light, and the narcissus filled the air with their rich scent. Swallows flew overhead.

Sudden tears came into Elaine's eyes. She bent over a narcissus flower to hide them, and breathed in the fragrance.

Raising her head, she said to the abbess, "It is here I would be surely. My heart is filled with such yearning."

"No, Elaine. You are not meant to be here. No more than at Caerleon."

"You advised last night…"

"And you refused. And it was well done. Your place is at Corbenic."

Elaine took in a deep breath.

"You may stay here as long as you will, and of course your will is free," the abbess went on, "but I cannot receive your vows, for it is clear to me your destiny is other."

"So be it," said Elaine.

They walked in silence.

"Tell me, Mother," Elaine said, "last night you called me the fisher king's daughter. Who is Pellehan to me?"

The abbess nipped back the tip of a rose plant. "Who am I to say? Suffice it that three events took place all the same year: Pellehan's wound and abdication of the throne, Pelles' marriage to your mother, and her death in your childbirth."

"My mother…"

"Was betrothed to Pellehan before his fatal wound, when, abdicating the throne, he yielded also his betrothed to his brother. Who had always loved her well; it is hard to say which of the brothers loved her more."

"Or which of the brothers fathered her child?" Elaine asked slowly.

A swallow alighted on the path before them. The abbess did not answer her question.

"Pelles mourned her greatly," she continued after a moment, "and he loves you dearly."

"Father or uncle, he loves me indeed as his daughter, that is not in question," Elaine said.

She leant to smell another narcissus, then added, "I asked Pellehan once. And he answered only, 'Mystery enshrouds the past, as it enshrouds the origins of the present, like the waters' depths from which the fish mysteriously arise; let mystery be.' Those were his words."

The bell for sext's noontime prayer rang.

Word was sent to Corbenic that the princess tarried at the Abbey yet a while more. Elaine passed the day working with one of the sisters in the herbal garden, spading the earth, preparing it for planting. One day flowed quietly into the next in the gentle rhythm of work and the nuns' prayers, her sleep threaded through by the sound of the night prayer bells.

The fourth night, she slept little and rose early for the predawn prayer. She walked up and down in the garden during the nuns' Chapter, returning to the chapel for terce and the mass which followed.

As she watched the priest hold out the bowl of wine

to the altar boy, who poured in the drops of water to mingle with the wine, her thoughts went to the tower chamber in Corbenic, where the golden grail stood on the altar. The image of the grail merged for her with the priest's bowl, as he raised paten and bowl in consecration. It was a special feast day so after the priest took the host and drank from the bowl, he also gave communion to the nuns, offering to each the white wafer that was the body of their Lord.

And the wine? Elaine wondered, her gaze resting still on the emptied bowl on the altar. Not white and round like a host, but flowing, fluid, spilling, staining... wine spilling forth as in life blood's flowing...swirling, flowing like a stream, like a falls.

The sky was filled with swallows as Elaine left the chapel after the concluding words of the *ita missa est*. She sent to have her horse made ready, and went to her aunt, telling her, "I return to Corbenic today."

ELAINE OF CORBENIC

CHAPTER 7

Spring's brief green was beginning to touch the gorse as she drew close to the coast after the morning's long ride through the wasteland moors that lay between the abbey and Corbenic's valley. It was in fact only the gorse which revealed spring, the gorse bearing golden flowers as if a grace of spring granted in token of the golden grail.

The lad whom the abbess had sent to accompany her niece on the return journey had family in Pointe Corbyne, so near the coast she took a different road than the way she'd come, one that passed by the seaside village. Once there, Elaine bid the lad take his leave, assuring him he need accompany her no further.

She passed by the churchyard with its great flat slab stone under which the serpent was said to writhe and flame fire; and disquiet welled in her. Quickly she cantered her horse until she was beyond the town, slowing to a walk as she rode on along the road. Then abruptly, craving the open vistas once more of the headlands before returning home, she turned off on a path which led up the slopes. She continued up toward the hills where some miles further east a narrow track led down through forest back into the valley and Corbenic's castle.

The horse stumbled, then limped a step or two. Elaine dismounted, and inspected his leg and hoof. The horseshoe had come off, she did not know how far back, and a sharp stone had gashed the hoof. The horse seemed to have twisted his leg in his stumbling.

"No trip down the steep path for you tonight, my friend," murmured Elaine as she held the injured hoof gently in her hands, then loosed it and stroked his back. "It's a warm evening. We'll rest on this slope tonight. The abbess sent no prior word of my return, so there will be no one to fret. If, on the morrow, you can't make it, I'll go alone and fetch help."

She walked him slowly to a level area of ground at the hill's crest, tethering him loosely on a sapling at the edge of the forest. The hour was late, and the sun golden on the pale grass, filling the air with soft diffuse light. Elaine walked a short way back down the slope to where two large boulders formed a gateway in the middle of the open hill, and a smaller rock against the left boulder made a seat. It was a favorite place of her younger years, a meeting place it had seemed to her, of the open sea's vastness and the hidden valley's mysteries.

The sun slipped steadily downward, red and burning, its light golden on the sea below. Golden like the grail chalice on Corbenic's altar. Above, the sky streaked crimson.

The vast yearning that the sea at times aroused in her filled her now, and called forth and mingled with the yearning she had experienced among the flowers at the cloister, and the inchoate feelings evoked by the emptied bowl's wine.

The sun slowly set into the sea, disappearing beyond the horizon.

Her eyes, as if by reflex, swept over to Pointe Corbyne where the dreaded serpent lay buried, then beyond to the barren countryside, and back to the darkening sea.

So many years, so many years, she thought. *And how many more? How long shall the land be barren, and dread shadow my being? How long the yearning in my heart? How long shall the golden cup hold its mysteries hidden?*

The darkness of night lay on the hill behind, only a last glimmer of light on the horizon over the sea. Elaine drew her cloak about her.

"I will not stir," she vowed to the twilight star bright in the deepening sky, "I will not stir until you hear my call. Heavens do you hear my voice? How long? Earth thirsts, is parched and barren: will you not grant it the rains of your mercy!"

Tears wet her face. She leaned her back against the stone behind her. The sea's sound was like the lament of her heart, a restless desire eluding words. The sky slowly settled into blackness, strewn richly with stars, except in the east where the moon, hidden yet behind the hill's crest, was beginning to wash the sky with its light.

Slowly, large and full, the moon reached above the trees, and suddenly her fear swelled up also, drawn like the tide to its fullness. The serpent's fire, the king's nonchalance, the fisher's wound, the distant crashing of the sea… Her breath would not come and she felt as if she would suffocate. Dream images crossed the sky of her fitful sleep: Morgana's mocking face, the serpent's coils, the bowl of wine, her horse's bleeding leg…and somewhere, under towering thunderclouds massing in the sky, a stream torrented along swirling rapids until, reaching a precipice, it plunged in silvery falls, a shimmering, liquid chalice…all the while a serpent coiled about her throat. Barely able to breathe, she called out.

When she opened her eyes again, the moon was high overhead, small like a wafer, round and full. She lay back against the earth, utterly spent.

Sleep came again and when Elaine awoke the moon was over the sea, large and white, its glimmer a long lance of light over the water. The sky was lightening, rose-tinged, the moon slowly descending toward the sea. The night's fear had dissipated, as if her call had been heard. There was a gentleness to the early morning air.

She watched the moon swell and sink—its largeness no longer ominous but now more like the swelling of a bud, of a womb's fullness—as it arced lower to finally dip into the sea. The sky was now pale blue and fully light. Sunlight sparkled on the sea and lay once again golden upon the hill below her, its bright mantle slowly spreading up the slopes, finally reaching the stones by which Elaine had taken refuge. As the warm light of the day spilled over her, her spirits lifted further. No secret had been yielded her, no answer from heaven, yet she felt the earth holding her gently, as it did all its morning offspring: rock and grass and shimmering spider web. A light sense of expectancy filled her.

She climbed again to the level area where her horse rested and examined the damaged hoof. "Still not healed, my friend?" she murmured. "Then wait here and rest more. When I return home, I will send one of the squires to you who has greater healing knowledge than I."

She left him and walked along the crest awhile, until she came to a deer path that led into the trees, then steeply down the forested slope into the valley below. Shadows lay thick, and the undergrowth was thorny, as if the valley wished to protect itself from intruders. She hitched her skirts at her girdle and started carefully down.

Chapter 8

She had rarely taken this path, for it was too steep and low-branched for horses. As she descended, the morning's gentle sunlight seemed far away, and the shadows lay heavy upon her. She remembered the abbess' words: that the grail was not only secret joy and longing, but the dark side of terror and dread, also.

At length she reached a stream, which flowed downwards into the valley. She followed the streambed, leaping from stone to stone, grasping roots and branches to steady herself. The way was less tangled now and gave easier passage. At last the stream fell in a small cascade, joining another stream to form a deeper channel on the valley floor. The trees here were lightly spaced, making a small clearing, and sunlight danced on the water. Her face and hands stinging with scratches, and hot from exertion,

Elaine knelt down to drink from the small, deep pool that the stream formed just beyond the falls.

She recognized the pool as one she had swum in as a child, coming to it back then from the valley path. Without bothering to look about, she slipped her gown and shift over her head, and dropped them along with her cloak on a large rock at the stream's bank. She stepped into the water, drawing in her breath sharply at its coldness. She swam a few strokes, then paused to shake the water from her eyes.

A thick serpent floated on the water in front of her, a dark shadow of undulating coils beneath the surface.

She gasped in terror, jumped from the pool, and looked back. Just a stick, she realized. Just a stick. But she slipped on her shift and gown, shivering. *Let fear seize you in its coils*, echoed Morgana le Fey's voice in her ears, blocking out the forest sounds, *let it suffocate you in its sweat*. And the minstrel's warning mingled with the curse, singing in the water's rippling: *beware the devourer of maidens, the serpent that comes to seize in its coils the fisher king's daughter, and bear away the grail treasure to the caverns of the sea...*

She felt a hand upon her shoulder. She looked up.

Kind, questioning eyes regarded her from a strong, scarred, though comely face. The hand was firm, and though she trembled still, she began again to breathe.

"What is it?" the stranger asked.

Tears welled into her throat and she could not speak at first. "Nothing," she uttered at last. "Only coils of fear...so tight I could not even breathe."

The stranger kept his hand on her shoulder. Reflecting back later, she found it surprising she had not been frightened by his sudden appearance, nor even by the possibility he'd been there all along. Absorbing the calm strength of his hand, her body slowly relaxed and the waves of fear ebbed away. Again the sounds of the forest reached her. She stood quiet beneath his hand a moment longer, oddly reluctant to move away, then drew back.

She saw him now entirely. Strong-shouldered, fair-browed, a smile upon his face, he was clad in hauberk and tunic, sword at his side. Against the tree behind him stood a shield of gold, its dark bar bearing three silver roundels.

"How foolish you must think me."

"No, my lady," he replied. "There is terror in life

indeed, and no shame to he—or she—who faces it."

The earth became more solid, the sky more clear. She heard a lark's song, and felt again the morning breeze. "I doubt you feel even a tremor of fear in the lists," she replied, "and I, at only a stick in the water, and words in my memory, am near suffocated in the vapors of fear."

"What manner of words?"

"Foolish ones I ought to have dismissed, coming from the shadows of dreams and minstrels' tales, of dark curses and fearsome serpents. Yet opening me to a terror that lies buried, unknown, unseen—a terror vaster than a dreamt curse, or the tale of a serpent. A terror that partakes of the immensity of the storm-clouded sky, the unknownness of time, and the heavy shadow of presentiment…"

"I can only share with you my warrior's knowledge," the knight beside her said quietly. "What you approach with fear will strike you down: any warrior bearing such a weight is lost from the outset. It is what one holds back from that looms large and fearful. But you can move forward, lightly, as if it were not so solid, as if swimming…*through* it…"

"Yet the waves of my fear are thunderous, dark and overwhelming…"

"Then yield to the waves. Dive into or beneath them. Let their force carry you as the surf bears the swimmer."

"Whither?"

"As lover yields to lover in darkness' passion, approach in trust destiny's kiss…" He picked up her cloak from the ground, and smiled at her. "Breathe gentle. Life bears you as stream and sea the fish: can a fish drown? Have no fear, my lady. Trust in the very darkness itself, in the secrets hidden beneath its terrors."

"You speak as one who knows water."

"Indeed," spoke the stranger, "and well I should, for my earliest mentor was of the lake."

She took the cloak he held out to her. "Swim onwards in trust I shall then, stranger. And I give you thanks for your words."

"Fairer or more courageous a swimmer I have never chanced upon," the knight said, picking up his shield, and added as he turned away, "Fare thee well, princess of the fishes' realm."

ELAINE OF CORBENIC

CHAPTER 9

Princess of the fishes' realm. *Odd words to choose by chance*, Elaine thought, as she walked on along the forest path, the murmuring of the stream loud in the morning air. *Odd words indeed from a stranger's mouth.*

She paused at the mossy bank where the path again arced close to the stream, and looked at the water, at the silver flickers among the rapids. *Fish, do you, in your own way, seek a grail's mystery in your flowing depths?* she wondered. *You who take the rapids with delight, the waterfalls with ecstasy?*

She looked back toward the low waterfall, gazing thoughtfully at the pool at its foot. On summer days, she had often come here. As a child she had jumped, then, a little older, dived, from the upper bank, skimming the cascade's foam into the water's depth, touching bottom and emerging with a glistening pebble in hand. Like a pearl diver. She could remember the fear before that first dive, as she had faced the foaming spray. And also the ecstasy of that dive, the startling shock of the cold water against her body; and its liquid caress, the bubbles foaming through her streaming hair. She remembered the underwater world meeting her open eyes, the undulating plants and quick darting fish, the pebble "pearls" large and glistening before her. She would' gather enough pebble treasures to fill the grail some day, or so had been her plan. Pearl diver of the woodland stream, bringer of pebble treasures to the grail...she smiled at the memory of her childish naiveté.

The pebbles had always disappeared from the grail. She had long believed her offerings had been taken up by heaven, the pebbles of the water's depth delighting the heavens even as their stars reflecting in the water surely delighted the stream.

Earth's pebbles and sky's stars, shared gifts from depth to height. And whoever it was who had removed the pebbles had had the tact to not rebuke or even mention it to the eager child.

Pebbles not unlike the roundels on the stranger's

shield.

So now it is another waterfall I am come to, she thought. *And terror's thunder and foam means simply that: another rapids to traverse, another falls to abandon oneself to, another depth to dive into, another unknown from which to bring back a precious pebble.*

"And is it not sung in the minstrels' tales," she said aloud to herself suddenly, "that sea serpents are but guardians of precious pearls?"

I came back, she whispered that evening, sitting in the grail tower room. *I came back.*

ELAINE OF CORBENIC

CHAPTER 10

The next morning, Elaine sat by the river, idly watching the fisher king in his skiff. She had not mentioned her encounter by the stream with the knight to him, nor to anyone, not even Heloise. It seemed now dreamlike, like one of the pebble pearls carried back by her younger self. Yet the words and metaphors of the stranger knight came to her mind now and again as her eyes rested on the sun's glimmering in the water, and her heart felt strangely warm.

How different this wild-rush–banked river edging the woods from the quiet, sun-soaked cloister of the abbey. Yet some intangible quality was shared; some shared knowingness, too, in both fisher and abbess, and she was content to learn that knowingness, whatever it was, here in Corbenic.

The fear had passed, had opened as the mist opens to the morning and dissolves away without sound. The sunlight was again warm, the sky no longer ominously heavy. The dragon serpent perhaps still writhed in its tomb in Pointe Corbyne, but the terror of the knowledge was gone. It no longer suffocated her dreams; she had left her terror that morning by the forest stream.

Pelles himself had ridden with her to tend to her horse on her return, revealing a healing knowledge and skill with the horse that she had not expected from him.

Her horse's leg was soon well enough that it could be ridden again and Elaine went out hawking one afternoon with Pelles and other members of the court. A mallard took flight before them, flushed out by the beaters and spaniels plunging through the bushes. Pelles unhooded his hawk. She watched the peregrine soar into the sky, tower above its quarry.

"A prize that bird," commented one of the courtiers. "Did you hear the tale of the hawk and the serpent?"

An old echo of fear hovered over Elaine as she watched the hawk drop down on the bird. She breathed and let the fear dissolve away, the memory of the stranger's hand on her shoulder still with her, and of the glance of his eyes. The dread was gone, and in its place lay an odd restlessness.

The odd restlessness stayed with her in the days that followed. She went each morning and evening as before to the grail tower, where she sat before the chalice, but within her she felt a strange emptiness which made her weep. All that had brought her happiness before now seemed flat and no longer moved her. Even the stream lost its allure for her and the woods seemed empty.

She took to going for long rides along the seacoast, the pounding of the breaking waves matching the rhythm of her restless pulse.

"Elaine, where are you?" Lady Breusen rebuked her one midmorning, looking over her shoulder and seeing Elaine had begun sewing with a red thread where it should have been gold.

Where am I? Elaine stared, abashed, at the crimson-threaded needle in her hand. *I am in a sunlit glen, a stranger's hand on my shoulder and his voice penetrating my heart.*

She took the gold thread and rethreaded the needle…

Day passed into day, each interminably slow. A

heaviness lay in the valley. Clouds heavy with moisture welled in the west coming from the sea, yet they did not let loose their rain.

CHAPTER 11

Elaine reined in her horse and stood on the headland crest, watching the waves break upon the shore below and the clouds mass on the horizon. Then slowly she turned her horse about, and quietly walked him along the sloping crest.

She had slipped away from Lady Breusen's summons to the embroidery frame with a plea to check on her horse. Once in the stables, she could not bear to return to close herself in the solar at her frame. "Tell Lady Breusen I will ride for a few minutes," she instructed the stable boy as she led out her horse. She had ridden along the river to the forest edge, then along a stream. The familiar sound of the water, once so calming, did little now to still her restlessness. The valley seemed too close about her, like a cloak outgrown. She felt a need for space, for the sea's wind to break through the hazed heaviness of the valley, and found herself again heading toward the path that led out of the valley to the hills by the coast. "Simply to see the sea and sky," she told herself, "then I will turn back."

In returning now, she took the gentler downward path that lay more southwest, in through the hills behind the coastal village. The hill sloped low to the protruding point pushing into the sea, and the huts and church spire of Pointe Corbyne appeared before her as she rounded the bend.

Pointe Corbyne, with its tomb where lay the fearsome serpent, and yet which habitually bore such a sleepy air. A sleepy air that seemed now abruptly startled awake. Everyone in the village seemed to have congregated in the church square, where a whirlwind of dust hid the focus of their attention. Now and again a spurt of flame sparked through the cloud of dust and smoke, and at times a glint of sun reflected as if off steel in the midst of the whirlwind. She wondered what scuffle was taking place in the village on this hazed, lazy day, but knew if there was aught of interest, she would hear of it later from Heloise, who was always knowledgeable about castle and village matters. She flipped the reins and turned her horse homeward.

In the past, entering the valley of the castle had always sent peace over her, like a cascade of clear water washing over her being, but this day there was no such greeting of peace. The air was oppressive, the dark clouds gathering over the hills, paused, pregnant, waiting.

Rains, break, she prayed, all the restlessness of her being filling her words. *Thunder, release. Earth suffocates in this closeness, this swollen heaviness. Rains, break loose, break loose.*

Back in the courtyard she dismounted. Pelles stood on the threshold of the great hall, speaking with a villager boy. A squire stood at the foot of the stairs, Pelles' horse at his side.

Pelles looked up, saw her, turned again to the boy, said more low words. Then they concluded their talk, and the boy took leave of him, descended the steps, passed Elaine with a courteous nod, and disappeared out the gate.

Pelles started down the steps, Elaine up them. They stopped where they met. "It was the priest's boy from the village," Pelles said; there was a seriousness on his face she was not accustomed to see. "A champion has come to

Corbyne. He fights the serpent. The battle has endured since morning."

The cloud of dust, with the spurts of flame, the glint of sun upon steel. *And I afraid no longer*, she thought. *The long year afraid, yet no one came, and now, when my own courage is won, the dragon serpent is battled.*

As if it had waited that.

"I ride to ask him to give us the honor of his presence at our table," the king said.

Elaine looked at him. That he who had denied even the serpent's existence should now accept the fact of the battle without comment did not seem, however, to warrant remark. Pelles started down the steps, and she accompanied him back down to where their horses stood. He took the reins his page proffered him, while she absently fingered her own horse's loose reins.

"There is no doubt as to the outcome?"

"It is the most valorous of Britain's knights who wields his sword against the serpent," Pelles said in response, heaving himself onto his mount. "He whose shield bears a fess sable charged with three roundels argents."

The three silver roundels. The lark's song mounting

into the sky, the sunlight shimmering on the morning dew of the forest clearing, the hand gentle and strong upon her shoulder, the shield against the tree. He, then, the one who had dispelled her fears at the waterfall. It was he confronting the serpent of the tomb.

Elaine stood without moving, watching Pelles as he wheeled his horse about and rode out through the gateway. As he disappeared from sight, the words of the abbess came back to her: "*Here shall come a leopard of king's blood, and he shall slay this serpent...*"

She handed the reins of her horse to the page waiting at her side, hardly seeing him as she slowly turned again to the stairs, an unaccountable lightness in her heart.

"Elaine! Where have you been? Your embroidery awaits." It was Lady Breusen, waiting for her on the threshold.

"Not now, Lady Breusen, sweet Mary, not now," Elaine said, brushing past her. Escaping to the tower stairwell, she entered the grail chamber, grateful for the quiet aloneness the room offered. She knelt before the ancient tarnished cup a long moment, then rose and went to the window and looked out at the moving clouds.

Moment by moment, word by word, the encounter by the stream replayed itself in her mind. The cloud of dust in Corbyne: *him.* Why had she not ridden down the slope? Why not take horse there now? The restlessness that had plagued her these twelve days, though, and had prompted her a hundred directions before was now utterly gone; in its place, a dream-like quietness. She had no need to take horse, ride to the coastal village, watch the roundels argents shielded knight wield his sword against the fiery serpent: She felt the encounter within herself, and knew with certainty of the knight's vanquishing of the serpent. There was no doubt in her, no more than had been in King Pelles. Only waiting.

A drop plinked on her nose. She looked up. A flash of lightning streaked over the hills, followed by a roll of thunder. The violet clouds in the distance, streaked now with gray rain and moving at last, were sailing into the valley. She leaned out and lifted her face to its first drops, felt the rain streak into her hair, splash against her face.

Earth welcomes you, she murmured. *The moor wastelands will drink you in great joy, and the dry lands surrounding receive you with thanksgiving. And the valley, the valley, too.*

A sheet of sunlight sliced through the cloudburst, and against the opposite slopes the fragment of a prism bridged sky to valley. Hardly a rain to turn the moor barrenness green perhaps, but on the rain-washed valley slopes the gorse's yellow glowed. The first rain of a long awaited spring.

ELAINE OF CORBENIC

CHAPTER 12

"Elaine, the king awaits you." Heloise lit a second candle in the darkening bedchamber, where she had just finished assisting Elaine dress for the evening meal. She regarded her lady questioningly.

Elaine broke her gaze away from the crepuscular-tinged hills, framed by the window arch, away from the faint evening star emerging into the rain-washed azure blue.

"Your hair is combed enough," Heloise added, smiling suddenly.

"I know. I..." Elaine laid aside her comb, giving a cursory look at her reflection in a small mirror of polished metal: its blurred image showed a maiden in a deep blue-green kirtle over a white tunic, a gold circlet on her flowing black hair. Rising, she cast a last glance through the window arch at the deepening blue, then passed through the doorway and down the stairwell.

He was standing with Pelles on the threshold of the hall, the roundels argents embroidered surcoat over a white tunic, sword at his side.

She hesitated at the stairway arch, she of free ways in woodland and seacoast, now suddenly shy.

Pelles called her name. She crossed the room.

"My daughter Elaine," he said to the knight at his side, and to Elaine, "My lord Launcelot."

Before her stood once again the one she had spoken with by the stream.

"Launcelot...Launcelot du Lac?" The stranger to whom she had revealed herself so intimately: Sir Launcelot du Lac? Arthur's brother-in-arms of whom the minstrel had sung. Britain's noblest knight.

Launcelot knelt before her, touched her hand to his lips. And she who had not recognized the name of the restlessness that had haunted her after their first encounter, nor of the happy expectancy that had buoyed her at the tidings of his return, now knew it, in her lilting joy at the kiss upon her hand, knew it with a deep plunging certainty, like a sword arcing to the depths of her heart.

"It is meet," Pelles said to Elaine, "that the grail be borne before the hall this night in honor of the day's deed."

Elaine inclined her head.

Starlight stippled the altar, softly glimmering on the golden chalice, as Elaine entered the ancient chapel. Three maidens of the court accompanied her, as was the custom for such more formal times when the grail was to be borne into the hall.

Her heart burning, she knelt a moment, then rose and took the cup in her hands. She stood quietly a moment, holding it before her. She felt its power in her fingers, as never before, felt it flow through her whole being. Were not the three maidens there to remind her, she might have remained there transfixed, forgetting altogether the waiting hall.

Gravely, tremulously, she bore the chalice to the hall, followed by the three maidens. It seemed to her she glided through a stillness fluid and silent like water, rather than walked upon stone.

She passed through the hall up to the dais and there paused first before King Pelles, then before Pellehan who reclined that night beside him on a couch, and held the grail for their reverence. Lastly she stood before the knight Launcelot. Her gaze remained focused upon the grail she held before him, its goldenness burning within her hands, and then, before passing on, her eyes raised a moment and met his. Silence enveloped the regard, a stillness as fathomless as death and as birth, as deep as the soul is deep, as if the grail swirled both hearts within its single hollow like a whirlpool flame. Time stopped and sound was no more. Yet it was an instant only, then Elaine lowered again her eyes, and departed from the hall.

She shortly returned, along with the maidens, having placed the grail back in its tower chamber, and took her seat at the left of King Pelles. A servant came with towel, ewer of water, and basin, and each washed their hands in the stream of poured water, drying them with the proffered towel. Grace was offered, and the servants entered, bearing bread and wine, soup, venison, and, to honor their guest, a special platter of chicken and rice boiled in almond milk, garnished with almonds and anise.

During the dinner Launcelot related how he had left

the King's court in Caerleon some weeks past. He made no mention of his encounter with Elaine, nor of having chanced upon the valley stream, but she understood from his narration that thence he had journeyed onwards along the coast. Finding no adventure, he had begun to return along the same route to Caerleon's court when, passing through the village of Pointe Corbyne, he had been accosted by a blind beggar who had called him by name and besought him to slay the dragon-serpent of the tomb.

As Launcelot had suffered slight wounds in his battle with the serpent, Pelles pressed him to remain at Corbenic some days before taking his departure. Courteously, he acquiesced.

ELAINE OF CORBENIC

CHAPTER 13

Elaine rode beside Launcelot, her falcon on her wrist. Refreshed after a morning of rest, Launcelot had joined the court in an afternoon's outing. The two rode slowly beside one another, eventually lagging behind the rest of the hawking party, hidden from them by the light mist settling in the valley. "Is it true," she asked him, "what the minstrel said? That you passed your youth under the tutelage of the Lady of the Lake?"

"It is as he said. It was she who gave me my name."

"Launcelot du Lac?"

"Yes."

"What then was your name of birth?"

"Galahad." He added, "It is an ancient name of our family. The first Galahad was the son of the Arimathean, and king of Wales. It was the Lady of the Lake who told me this, and many other things."

"Tell me of what it was like there."

"I did not swim with fishes," he laughed. "It was a lake of magic, a place of watery enchantment. Yet true, stone was not solid. One could find within it an infinity of space and a whirlwind of energy. One moved more gracefully, fluidly, more as through water than through air, and more in play than in deadly earnest."

"Then how was it for you to leave your magical watery realm to come to Arthur's court?"

"It was a return to my native world. Gladly did my hands grasp the heavy metal of the sword given me, and gladly did I mount the solid back of the weighty destrier provided. A world of solid stone and solid flesh."

Sunlight broke through the mist, an evening sunlight, casting a golden translucent hue unto the grass.

Launcelot reined in a moment. "Yet there is left...at times...an echo..." A peregrine, Pelles' perhaps, soared high above them, the golden sunlight flashing on its outspread wing. "...a memory or awareness," he continued. "Yet, not even so direct. In the midst of all this solidity—not in the moments of battle, sword against sword, blood hot and breath heavy, cries and dust mingling, nor in moments of passion, but somewhere in the space afterward, after the moment of victory and before the next summons, between the satisfaction and the desire, about me quieted dust, stone, dried blood, lifeless corpses; or at Caerleon, body reclad, amidst the glitter and cold intrigue of the court—some trace of memory echoes through it all of that other world, of that fluidity of space..."

Launcelot broke off abruptly and laughed. "What nonsensical words I speak!" He fell quiet, flicked his rein and the horse began walking again, Elaine's following alongside.

He smiled ruefully. "I have never tried to speak of it to anyone before," he said. Not even to Guinevere. She would tease about such words, or would perhaps have been jealous of the Lady of the Lake. But with the raven-haired princess riding at his side—one moment a wild stream nymph, and the next, mysterious, majestic grail bearer—it seemed natural to share these long-submerged secrets. She moved in a valley world where spirit interfaced with matter, and sacredness lay hidden beneath each stone. With her, something sparked in him—as if she were a fisher delving the depths of his soul.

"Your valley itself is surely an enchanted one," he said, to change the focus. "I had heard of Castle Corbenic, perhaps from the Lady of the Lake herself, but as no one I knew had ever come across it, truth to tell, I did not know if it were real or no."

"How did you come to these environs?" she asked.

"I was lost on my way."

"And where was your way?"

"To the seeking of adventure." His face hardened.

"And what led you forth to seek it?"

He frowned, then catching her eyes, relaxed and laughed. "To be frank, a quarrel with the queen."

"Do you love her then?"

"I am her champion. All Britain knows."

"I know," she acknowledged, then repeated her question. "Do you love her?"

"Yes." Launcelot answered without hesitation, his voice quiet.

Neither spoke for a while as they rode onwards.

"Is she as beautiful as they say?" asked Elaine, at length.

"Even more beautiful, my lady."

CHAPTER 14

That night, in great solemnity, Elaine again bore the grail through the great hall when all were gathered to sup. When she reached Launcelot, her step faltered. The grail felt heavy in her hands, heavy like the earth. *This surely is he*, she thought then, *the one who is come to win the grail's secret to Britain.*

She sat by Launcelot during the meal, and the grail's aura, which enveloped her, cast a certain beauty upon her which the knight had never before beheld, and which riveted his attention. A solemnity was wrapped about her that made it difficult to see her as the same elfin princess he had ridden with during the day—a solemnity different and yet as real, and more impenetrable, than even the queen's.

With morning, though, all aura of solemnity had

disappeared and Elaine was racing Launcelot with childlike laughter as they rode through the valley, she having undertaken to acquaint the visitor with Corbenic's surroundings. They spent the day together while the king held council, having entrusted his visitor to the princess.

"The grail," Launcelot said, as they slowed their horses to a gentler amble. "What is it? It holds one in its power; it draws one."

"It is said to be Christ's cup, which he shared with his friends the night before his death. And which, legend says, caught the blood and water that later spilled from his pierced side. It is a relic held in our family for long generations."

Launcelot's face revealed reverence. "Though the Lady of the Lake spoke to me once of King Pelles of Lystenois, she did not speak of the grail. How is it that so holy a relic remain hidden in so far a valley? Surely its presence and grace would bring glory and greatness to all of the realm."

"There is one who will come, it is said," Elaine answered him, "whose quest it is to bring the grail to Britain." She added, "If Britain be ready."

Launcelot said nothing.

That night a third time she bore forth the grail in procession through the hall, and when she passed before Launcelot, she held a strange foreknowledge she would bear the grail in her hands no more.

ELAINE OF CORBENIC

CHAPTER 15

Launcelot stood against the parapet, looking eastward. The rising sun bathed Corbenic's valley in light. It was Guinevere, though, who filled his thoughts, even as she had filled his night dreams, her smile blinding like the sun, her green eyes beckoning. Guinevere…who was still angry at him for having hesitated before climbing into the ignoble pillory cart that would allow him to more swiftly deliver her from Meliagrance, the dark lord who had abducted her. Who had not herself seemed entirely without enjoyment at her enforced stay with the dark lord. Guinevere, Guinevere, Guinevere.

It was not simply her impetuous anger that had impelled him to leave the court: it was having witnessed Arthur's reaction to the abduction. The king loved her, and if Arthur's involvement with Britain left him little time for pleasantries with her, he loved her still with as innocent and full a love as when he had first chosen her as his bride—against Merlin's counsel chosen her as the only one he would make his wife and queen—and sent Launcelot to escort her to court.

Ill-fated Arthur's choice of escort had been. Being with Arthur when he had heard the story of Meliagrance had made Launcelot vividly conscious of Arthur in a way that was easier to avoid when the king was occupied with affairs of state, as was his wont, Guinevere maintaining that the country alone mattered to him, so that she and Launcelot were betraying no trust when they slept together.

It had been that: the look on Arthur's face when he had heard the news, the cry of concern that flew from his lips not for his honor but for the queen's safety, and the expression in his eyes when Guinevere was returned safely to him. With that fresh in his mind, how could he touch Guinevere's face without seeing Arthur's? If perhaps he had been able to talk with Guinevere…but when he had broached the subject with her she had burst into remonstrance about his momentary hesitancy to climb into the pillory cart used for transporting criminals when the driver had offered to lead him to Guinevere. Even Sir Gawain, his companion, had refused to tarnish his knight's honor by traveling in such an ignominious manner. That Launcelot had chosen to proceed despite the shame of doing so had little import for the queen. She had screamed at him, and would not hear him, ordering him from her sight. The cart perhaps was not the issue. Perhaps it had been her own feelings of guilt—toward Launcelot, not Arthur. Would Meliagrance have abducted her if she had shown no hint of favor toward the dark lord?

Launcelot regarded the fisherman on his boat in the distance below, through the morning mist that still hung over the water. How quiet, calm, this provincial castle, the only sounds the morning songs of swallows flying from their nests below. How distant from the intrigues and entanglements of the royal court.

A plague upon her! Could he not get Guinevere from his thoughts? They were done with one another, surely. Yet if she sent for him, would his resolve be able to stand? Ah Guinevere, Guinevere...

He felt a presence at his side, so silent an approach

he had not heard her.

"My father says you return to Caerleon on the morrow."

"As God grants, princess."

"Your presence will be lacked, my lord."

She wore a fuchsia kirtle; her hair billowed wild in the wind. Like a wild rose, he thought. If Guinevere was an intricately petaled, blood-red rose—rich, regal, seductive, velvet, perfumed, Guinevere oh Guinevere— this youthful maiden, innocent, open and wide-eyed, was a wild rose, simple fragrant petals open to the sun.

He smiled at her.

Salt dew swelled tremulously in her eyes.

He reached and took it on his finger. "Elaine..."

She shook her head with a rueful smile and looked away, looked toward the fisherman on his boat. They stood in silence, side by side.

The fisherman drew in his line. The speck of fish at its end flashed silver in the sun.

"It may be that he is my true father," Elaine said, as if to introduce a new note into their speech, but her voice thoughtful. It was as if she were trying out the statement.

"The fisherman?"

"He was a king. Did you know that?" Elaine's voice was liquid and distant. She went on. "He was king of all this land once. His name is Pellehan. He sat at table the night of your arrival." Ordinarily the fisher king kept to himself, dining with the court only on the great feast days of the year. His presence at table that night had surprised Elaine, and caused her wonder.

"Years ago he was wounded by a spear. It left him changed, they say. It was about the time drought hit the surrounding lands. He took the weight of it onto himself. He took to his little fishing boat. Had no more time to give to court and royal trivialities, he said. All day long, he fishes in his little skiff. He left the duties of the kingdom to his brother, Pelles. That is when Pelles became grail keeper."

Again, the grail, Launcelot thought. This thread of the grail, of mystery, appeared again and again. Grail, fishermen who were kings...and a wild rose maiden chanced upon in a stream, bearer of the grail and daughter of a fisher king.

"The duties of the kingdom, the grail...and you?"

"Perhaps."

Launcelot remembered the morning when he had

first seen her swimming in the stream, black hair swirling in the bubbly water, naked and wild as a fish. Between the robust, fatherly King Pelles and the strange, solitude-choosing fisher, he would lay his wager she came indeed from the latter's seed.

A gust of wind blew toward them from across the parapet wall.

"Come, let us go down to the shore, and see if he has a fish for us to breakfast on," Launcelot said, in a sudden light mood.

Elaine looked at him, laughed. "I shall be swifter than you, old war horse," she mocked him, and turned, running to the stairwell. Launcelot followed.

At this hour at Caerleon, he thought, all would be assisting at mass, and afterwards, the queen and her ladies breakfasting in their garden...and in this hidden, mist-filled strange valley I break fast with a fisher king's daughter on the bank of a river.

Dew wet their shoes as, moments later, they made their way through the rushes along the stream leading to the river bank, Launcelot now in the lead. Light beams streamed through the morning mist and through the boughs overhanging the river, making dappled patterns on Lancelot's surcoat. Following him, Elaine felt as if she herself were the stream, for within her there seemed to be waterfall where her heart should be, liquid cascading waterfall.

Near where the stream flowed into river, the fisher king sat in his skiff, holding his line. Though their footsteps were muted in the moss and his back to them, he turned at their approach. Eyes old and deep as the river sparkled at them from the weather-beaten face, its deep-cut lines like hills softened by time.

"So," he said. "Welcome." He nodded to the bank where coals smoldered in a heap. "Your breakfast awaits you."

Launcelot looked at the fisher king. He looked at the fish, shimmering silver in the morning rays in the old man's hand, and at the smoldering coals. What had been a simple jest seemed to have been given reality at face value in this hidden valley.

"Knight of the lake, tend to the coals," continued the old man, interrupting Launcelot's musings. "Elaine, come take the fish."

Elaine slipped off her shoes and hose, gathered her skirts up and hitched them up unto her girdle. She waded out over the pebbles to the skiff, the water eddying about her hem. Her eyes were filled with questioning, a new shyness on her face.

The fisher king said nothing right away, a gentle smile in his eyes. Then at last, as if in answer to her unspoken feelings, "It is meant."

"But old one, can I still serve the grail and..." she stopped, then tried again. "Heart and body and soul I yearn for Launcelot—yet heart and body and soul I am bearer of the grail. Old fisher, what must I do?"

"What does your heart bid you?"

"Deeper than life, deeper than love, my will is to serve the grail."

"It is meant, child. The grail is served in more than one way. Does not scripture say there is a time for everything under the sun? A time to embrace and a time to refrain from embracing, a time to bear and a time to yield, a time to sow and a time to harvest, a time to be born and a time to die? You have borne the grail. Now your call lies in a different kind of bearing."

"They say, and I well believe, he is the noblest knight of Britain," Elaine said. "Is it not he who shall bring the grail to Britain?"

"Perhaps, little one, but not as you may imagine."

"Old one, there is foreboding in me, oh, so great a foreboding."

"Go and prepare the fish," he said only, placing the silver fish into her hands.

She took the fish and returned to the shore, where she laid the fish among the coals Launcelot had stoked. And together, that morning, the two broke fast upon the fish given them by the fisher king.

ELAINE OF CORBENIC

CHAPTER 16

That afternoon Launcelot went with Pelles to the hunt. Elaine watched from the stairs of the keep as they set off, declining to accompany them, not trusting that she could make merry and light with everyone when her heart was so otherwise.

When the horses had disappeared through the gate, she turned back inside the castle and, evading her maidens and Lady Breusen, climbed the stairs to the grail chamber. The fisher king's words interwove through her thoughts and echoed through her mind, diverse feelings and musings intermingling within like the dust motes playing in the sunbeams as she sat in the room's quiet, along with sadness at Launcelot's impending departure. Peace eluded her, and restless, she took leave of the tower chamber to take some air in the garden.

As she crossed the courtyard, the sun still high in the afternoon sky, she encountered Pelles.

"You did not go?" she asked.

"I returned early. I had a matter to attend to." He looked at her. "I have sent a man after the hunt with a message for Launcelot from the queen, with her ring as token, that he meet her this night at the castle of Case. I sent Launcelot's shield and sword with the man, that he might go direct, if he so choose."

"So suddenly gone—how can it be?" Her eyes betrayed her bewildered disbelief. She turned her face away. It could not be. From Pellehan's words she had thought, had dared to hope, yet that now there should not even be a parting, no final words...

"Sire, allow me to ride to Case, that I may bid Sir Launcelot farewell."

"It will be well done," Pelles nodded gravely without pause, as if such had been his idea all the while. "Array yourself well; take the Lady Breusen to accompany you, and a party of knights for escort. Take your farewell of Launcelot and return in the morning."

Preparations were hastily made and the horses readied, and within the hour Elaine, accompanied only by

Lady Breusen, along with a small retinue of knights, set out for the castle of Case.

As they travelled, a medley of thoughts and feelings vied within the princess. One moment she was dismayed at the temerity that had prompted her to propose so foolish an excursion. How could Pelles have granted such a request? It was the queen Launcelot had ridden to rendezvous with; her arrival would surely be untimely. The next moment all else was eclipsed by the heartfelt urgency of seeing Launcelot one last time—and if indeed she would see him no more, to have at least a word of farewell.

At last the castle of Case loomed in the distance on a slight rise of land, a narrow moat surrounding the outer walls of the square keep. As they passed through the gatehouse into the bailey, she saw no sign of the queen's retinue, nor of Launcelot's horse. The castle's steward, who was waiting for them in the courtyard, greeted them courteously. Lady Breusen exchanged words with him, and he led them to an upstairs chamber, where water was brought for the princess to wash away the dust from her journey.

"I will perhaps have a glimpse of the queen, when she arrives," Elaine mused as Lady Breusen helped her dress after she had bathed.

"No," said Lady Breusen. "She will not be here."

"A new message? But then Launcelot..."

"Is still on his way."

"I wonder that he is not yet arrived. If he went straight from the hunt..."

"He would have returned first to your father's hall, to take leave of his royal host."

"Then it is oddly done, that I am come here to bid him farewell. Yet Pelles..."

"Sent you here in wisdom. Sit, let me comb out your hair."

CHAPTER 17

The quarry of the chase at Corbenic that afternoon had been a great deer, and it was Launcelot who took it. As he and the others were resting their horses, the messenger carrying the queen's ring arrived. When Launcelot heard his words and saw the ring, his face revealed much emotion and he hastened back to the castle. The hunt had led them some distance, and by the time he reached the castle, afternoon shadows had lengthened. "I thank you for your hospitality," he bade Pelles, "but I must take my leave this very afternoon. The queen summons me to the castle of Case. As I understand, not far from here."

Pelles inclined his head in acknowledgement, saying, "I will have my manservant prepare you water to bathe, so that if you will, you may first wash away the mud and sweat of the hunt." Once bathed and properly appareled for his rendezvous with the queen, all hastily accomplished, Launcelot set out from Corbenic without further delay.

With mixed emotion and eagerness Launcelot rode to the castle of Case. The deep blue of twilight had fallen about him as he approached the castle. A sliver of new moon arced over the evening star.

It was not Guinevere, but Elaine, oddly enough, who came to his mind as he glimpsed the moon's slender arc. As he crossed over the drawbridge and entered the castle gates, however, his thoughts turned again to his rendezvous with the queen. He dismounted, handing his horse to a waiting squire.

Lady Breusen met him on the threshold of the great hall; in his haste, he did not stop to wonder at her presence.

She offered him a cup of wine to take away the dust of the journey.

He downed the wine. "The queen?"

"She is not here."

"Sacré..."

"She will not be here. A messenger came earlier.

She will not come. She awaits you rather at Caerleon, for your return."

"God knows my blood is hot enough now to ride on to Caerleon this very night, but my horse deserves more consideration than my fickle majesty." There was anger in his voice.

He held his cup out to her. "Pour me more wine."

When he had downed a second cup, then a third, Lady Breusen led him upstairs, showed him to a chamber and left.

He opened the door.

A woman stood looking out the window, her back to him. She was clothed in blue and azure interfaced with rose, her black hair tumbling loose. It was not Guinevere.

She turned at the sound of the door opening.

"I had thought to find the queen here," Launcelot began.

"No." Elaine's lips trembled as she spoke the single word. She wore no jewelry. The open neckline revealed the young throat he had once glimpsed wet in the stream from a distance. A quality like the moistness of dew lay upon her, yet in that moment he saw that she whom he had thought child was also woman.

"I came to say farewell."

Launcelot looked at her. "You must have left before me, to have reached here before me," he said, slowly as if trying to unravel a knot.

"Yes, my lord."

Launcelot crossed the room. A draft of wind fanned the flames of the room's candles, and he closed the window's heavy wooden shutter, turned again toward her. They stood so close, it was as if he could hear her very breath.

Her eyes were fathomless, liquid as the lake whence had come his name. His fast-paced ride to the castle, the queen, even the chamber walls fell away from his awareness as he met her gaze. Wide her eyes, moist like the deer of the morning's hunt, deep and full.

"Elaine."

Launcelot. She did not speak it aloud but the name resonated from her heart throughout her being, drew him closer, drew him as the lodestone draws the pole star.

Launcelot. She felt his hand upon her face, such gentle a touch she'd never have guessed of so strong a hand and her face softly surrendered to the tenderness of his fingers.

Time and space yielded. The night opened infinitely deep. Stone floor gave way to lake bed, clothes gently drifting away, as she slowly fell, slowly somersaulted in his arms upwards through space.

She held him to her, received him into her. *Launcelot, Launcelot. Galahad of the lake, oh, my Launcelot...* arcing, coursing as the falling star, falling, falling into the lodestone, into the depths of the lake.

ELAINE OF CORBENIC

CHAPTER 18

Launcelot woke first. He rose from the bed and opened the window, and morning light flooded the room.

He stared at the young woman lying in the bed he had risen from as if he had never seen her before, her dark hair swirled over the pillow and her bare shoulders as she breathed gently, peaceably in sleep.

Turning away, he reached for his clothes.

The quiet sounds of his movement awoke her. She opened her eyes, saw him nearly clad. "My lord..."

"I must go back to court."

She sat up, drawing the covers about her. "When will you return?"

Launcelot gave a low laugh which held no lightness. "I will not return."

Letting the covers fall from her, she rose, went over

to him, placed a hand on his arm. He shook his head gently, lifting her hand off. She stood before him, young, naked, eyes wide, puzzled.

Moved despite himself, Launcelot drew her to him, kissed her gently on the lips, then released her.

He bent to fasten his boots.

Gently, softly like a feather, she felt her heart fall through space.

Launcelot finished the one boot, turned to the other. She knelt beside him, touching his knee. "Launcelot." The intensity of her voice forced his gaze to lift and meet hers. "Last night…"

"It was not meant." The words came out with heavy force, each like an ax stroke. Reluctant to bear her gaze, he shifted his to the window, and added, his words quick, "I lost leave of my senses."

Elaine stood.

Launcelot straightened. He took up his sword belt and buckled it on.

"It *was* meant." Her voice was low, fluid, like the stream.

"Elaine, Elaine, forgive me, it was not," said Launcelot. "I do not know what possessed me." He took his cloak from the chair where he had let it fall the night before, clasped it on.

With the briefest of genuflections, without meeting her eyes, he left.

She stood in the empty room, still naked. She stared at the empty bed, covers flung back and draping to the floor, then lifted her eyes to the window. A meadowlark flew by and its morning song stirred life into her. She wiped the tears from her face with the back of her hand.

It had been meant. Only that, she knew.

ELAINE OF CORBENIC

CHAPTER 19

Corbenic was forever different, from that day forth.

An emptiness seemed to fill the valley like mist. A strange hollowness cupped time, like the hollowness of the chalice. She felt like the sea foam washed up on the shore and left glistening on the empty sand as the waves which carried it there draw back with the retreating tide.

The days passed long, and she forgot what she had filled them with before. The sky was empty, the birds' song muted, the colors of the gorse washed out. Her lute strings sounded off tune, and no matter how she turned the lute's pegs, they seemed not to find their key.

Her very body ached for him.

She walked often on the ramparts, eyes reaching out beyond the river below and out over the valley, as if watching for the cloud of dust of an approaching horseman.

She waited for his return. No part of her would believe his words, would believe that by the time he reached Caerleon he would not turn his horse and come back to claim her as his love.

He must come back, she thought. *He must. The grail waits still in its chamber. The land is still wasted. Did not the rains break one brief moment the day of his coming? Was that not an omen, a harbinger of good things to come?*

He *must* come back. With him at her side, the unknown held no shadow, mysteries could be penetrated, and joy found. His coming had been for her a premonition of fullness, like the faint traces of the rainbow fragment that threaded the sky during the rain's dispersion. It was not possible that he would not return, that she would have to raise herself up, and, burdened with the new knowledge of what it could be like to share with another, regather the threads of life alone.

She said to Pellehan with accusing eyes, with rebellion, "Did you not say it was meant? How can what was meant be so easily unspun?" She had joined him in his skiff moored to the willow tree at the river's bank, sitting a long time silent before the words spilled forth.

Pellehan regarded her with compassion. "How? Why? Child, you are not the first to ask such questions."

"Tell me, old one," she cried angrily.

"What took place, took place," Pelles said simply. "And it cannot be unspun."

"Took place, yes, a wine of joy emptied as quickly as the fullness of a cup. And now the cup is empty. No, now it is filled with the wine of pain."

"It is the same cup," said Pellehan. "The same emptiness which is called fullness and fullness which is called emptiness. As when water is mixed with wine, how can you separate pain from joy, joy from pain?"

Then Elaine said no more, only hid her face in her hands, and wept.

ELAINE OF CORBENIC

CHAPTER 20

Although finally she began to realize Launcelot would not return, she could not uproot a defiant hope. Yet though clouds of dust approached now and then, it was never he, nor even a messenger. Once when she entered the hall, Elaine saw at the far end a knight, broad-shouldered, in white surcoat, his back turned to her. Her breath stopped and her heart beat fast, but then he turned and it was not he. How could it have been he, who was at court in Caerleon-on-Usk, and by his own words not like to come again to Corbenic?

The hall was filled for her now only with empty babbling, tinny laughter. Certain nobles, newly aware of her burgeoning womanhood, pressed their attentions on her. It only made her grieve the more: *Why these, when it is Launcelot I yearn for?* And she was short in dismissing them.

At times she turned angrily against herself, that she could not banish him from her mind. She cursed her powerlessness over her own feelings, and over his for her. Yet her heart was not under her control.

The days slowly passed into weeks.

During that time, Pelles gave the keeping of the grail to a certain hermit, while his masons might repair an arch that had been crumbling, restore the chamber, create more artfully the vault above, and in all ways make the tower room a more fitting domicile for the grail.

In the process of their work, the masons uncovered an opening that led into a small, ancient chapel long forgotten, for after the castle's construction, a larger chapel had been built by the gatehouse in the courtyard. The chapel, despite its size, was flawless, its stone arches graceful, and it was decided to make it the new repository of the grail. The grail was brought and set upon a silver altar, and covered with a cloth of red samite.

The grail she would no longer carry. Tradition required that the bearer at the high feast processions be the fairest maiden of the valley, untouched of man, and she had yielded her maidenhood to Launcelot. She was no longer that one.

She was bereft of both future and past. The thread of her life—the grail, its mysteries and promise—had been taken from her. She could not re-enter time to return to the world that had once been hers. The past, that world, lay now like the garden's entrance barred by the angel's sword. The grail was hidden from her beneath its shroud of samite; all that had been the focus of her life before was lost, misted in dimness. And the one to whom she had offered her future was gone and would not return. Emptiness faced her from both heaven and earth.

ELAINE OF CORBENIC

CHAPTER 21

One day a traveling minstrel came to Corbenic. He bore news from surrounding lands, and rumors of impending war in France. Of Arthur's court, he said all was well. The damask-attired ladies, he sang, were like blossoms of the fairest flowers among which Guinevere was the most fair; the knights were valiant, and brave their adventures. Elaine, despite herself, remained in the hall the nights the minstrel tarried at Corbenic, listened to his tales and songs. The names were by now familiar to her: Gawain, Gareth, Percivale de Galis, Ector and, oh, too familiar, Launcelot.

One night, after the king had left the hall at the settling in of darkness, and knights and servants alike were bedding down to sleep, a handful of the younger knights and ladies, among them the princess, remained seated by the minstrel to hear a few last strums. Soon even these departed, all but Elaine, Heloise and a couple other ladies-in-waiting. The minstrel in weariness set aside his lute, stood and stretched, preparing to take his leave. Elaine, though, to whom sleep came late these nights, entreated him for yet one last song.

And so he sat himself down, took up and strummed again his lute. He sang a lay of a fair maiden who had loved the knight Launcelot years ago when he was young, had won of him that he bear her favor in the tournament that he fought the next day, and when he never returned, had died for love. Her dead body had been floated down the river in a barge to Caerleon-on-Usk, with a letter in her cold hand proclaiming herself the unhappy lover of the knight. The maiden's name was Elaine, and though the minstrel named her daughter of the lord of Astolat, Elaine, listening, did not know in truth in the dim evening candlelight whether he spoke of another or of herself in a different time and a different place.

When the minstrel had finished, Heloise, who was ignorant of what had passed between the princess and Launcelot, sighed, "Ah, what a sad song. Such ill-fated love."

"No," said Elaine, rising. "Such strong love, stronger than the beloved's indifference."

"Indeed," said the minstrel to Heloise and Elaine alike. "If love has any meaning at all, it must bear more weight than the hazards of fate. What meaning has it if it lies so dependent on its return or no? Is love a beggar?"

The song stayed with Elaine that night, slept with her, was with her when she woke. Even as she assisted at the morning's mass, it remained with her. She could imagine it well:

The maid descending the last curve of the stairway, her vision opening into the hall. The stranger standing with her father, broad-shouldered, dark-locked, noble-browed, with sword, yet without shield. A burning inside her, as if a coal had been dropped into her heart.

Her father, seeing her, nodding for her to approach, saying "My daughter Elaine, my lord," to the stranger at his side. The latter smiling at her, and the coal burning more intensely as if flamed by a breath's blowing.

"Your daughter is fair," the knight saying graciously. All too graciously, for the coal burst into flame in the heart of the lord of Astolat's daughter.

The priest finished his reading of the scripture

passages and moved to the altar. He took the cup, poured in the wine and water, and proceeded with the offering and consecration. During the prayers for the departed that followed, Elaine silently whispered the maid of Astolat's name.

The mass ended and Elaine left the chapel with the rest. Pausing by the arched window in the stairwell as she returned to her chambers, she looked out toward the river. "But I, I shall not lie down and die," she quietly vowed.

All week long Elaine's thoughts returned to the other Elaine—that other Elaine who, undaunted by his blindness to her love, had called herself Launcelot's lover. That and simply that: his lover. One who loved him. Unto death. Not loved by, not wed by, nothing given to. But loving. Simply by the power of her heart, loving.

"His lover." She repeated the maid of Astolat's words. Tried out the sound, took them for her own, gave them her own meaning.

The clarity of her voice sounded loud in her own ears. "Yes," she repeated to herself, "now and always his lover. Never his wife perhaps, never his beloved. That lies with him. Only for this am I answerable: this battle-scarred, gentle, generous knight, I loved. My love is given to him—and what I have given I do not take back."

Nor do I ask anything of you, she thought. *What I have cannot be taken away. Your hands upon my face, the night shared—these are still real. The gift of your words that first morning by the stream, the confidences shared while our falcons flew, the fish partaken together, the encounter of our eyes when I bore the grail before you that first night—all these* are *now and forever. I bear their fullness within me.*

Still, proudly as she might walk, loneliness lay upon her where before there had been none. Sleep eluded her no longer, indeed called her more often, as if to heal her with dreams. But she had little desire for food. It was as if the pain of her emptiness had passed into her body, little waves of grief welling within her belly, and an ache swelling her breasts.

It was some time before she realized that the welling was not of grief but of new life.

ELAINE OF CORBENIC

CHAPTER 22

Her hand touched her belly in wonder, in joy. *Their fullness within me,* she repeated to herself in awe, as she walked along the stream in the early morning sun.

"You thought to take your love back?" she murmured softly, her hand still resting on her abdomen as she sensed the stirrings of life within her. "To deny it as only an enchantment? An enchantment then heavy and substantial. It weighs, oh, it weighs in my womb, and ere the year is out, its voice will sound aloud, it will walk upon this earth.

"I bear your love in my womb, solid, substantial. No longer only in my heart, but in my very body. It moves, it kicks. Your life has sent forth root into my being. Your life draws my own into itself, swirling within me. Whatever may become of you or me, like pods carried on separate winds, your life entwined with mine grows—soon to fountain forth a new being beneath these very skies."

The new-found joy, the secret ecstasy, filled her for days. She shared it with no one at first. Yet her hand as if by its own accord moved to her belly when no one's eyes were upon her, making little circles on its beginning roundness, a gentle smile on her lips.

Then one day the realization truly hit her that she was with child—and alone.

She would not have Launcelot wed her for honor's name when his longing was for another. Nor was it likely he would even make the offer. Other men had sired bastard children; the shame was left with the woman.

Her roundness would soon make her a mockery to the court: There goes one who slept with a knight who serves another. A knight who had gone to the castle of Case, expecting that other. Had the queen even indeed sent word? Or had the ring been a deception? And if a deception, why and wherefore she could not fathom. In the end, it mattered little which it had been, or why. She could hear the priest's voice preaching God's disapprobation for those trespassing the church's laws of matrimony. Would heaven regard her ill, who had lain with a man and bore now his child without the church's sacrament?

All that was within her immediately answered: No. Deception though the night might have been, it had held no lack of sacredness. No ring perhaps, yet had not the sharing of the fish been in its own way a sacramental meal?

That night a wind of terror came over Elaine. She had heard tales of childbirth before, of the pain and the agony. Her own mother had died in childbed. "Birthing is painful and bloody work," Lady Breusen had once told her. "It surely requires more capacity to bear pain, and more courage, than is asked of the knight going into the lists, or into battle. Yet it is said if you go with the waves of pain, breathe into them and flow with them, the pain is bearable." As she remembered these last words, Elaine drew herself tall. How could she doubt her capacity for pain and for courage was any less than that of a knight in the lists? In this, she would prove herself the equal of Sir Launcelot. She remembered his words by the stream that morning of her fear—on diving into the waves, letting their force carry one as the surf bears the swimmer. And she smiled softly.

She did not know whom to tell, but tell someone, sometime, she must. She did not want to grieve Pelles, nor become the cause of ill feeling or bartering between the courts. Hours of peace and joyous delight shared the days with hours of desperate tears and bewilderment. For now, the fullness of her gown hid the growing roundness, and she kept her silence, as week passed into week.

CHAPTER 23

She was standing near the entrance of the garden one evening, hand cradling her belly, troubled and low in spirit, when she sensed someone behind her. She turned. It was Sir Bromwell.

"Lady Elaine," he began. "I am perhaps the most powerful noble of your father's land, the most proven, an old friend from days past. Though I have no royal title, I have wealth, power and skill of arms. I have also fidelity: I would take no paramour, my heart is not given to another man's wife. I would provide well for you, honor you, provide a name for…"

"My lord, no!"

He took a step closer, clasped her arm. "Elaine, think. What will you do? You cannot have Launcelot: He does not love you. You must know that. What else have you in mind? Enter a convent, big-bellied?"

Elaine wrenched her arm free and turned away, furious, but he turned her again toward him, took hold of her face, kissed her lips. The touch of a man other than Launcelot felt repugnant beyond endurance, though her mind whispered, *He speaks truth.* Tearing herself away from him, she ran into the privacy of the garden, passing through the bare orchard trees bordering its low walls, and between the hedges surrounding the raised herb beds, to the well at the garden's center, leaned against it, and wept.

So he knew. Her secret must be apparent to all.

No future seemed possible. Launcelot indeed would have none of her. Yet was her heart given to him, and what was given not so easily recalled. She would be wife to no other man: she could not be wife to one man when her heart had been given already to another. Even for honor, or to render happy the lord Bromwell—stocky, good-natured Bromwell who had always been fond of her —or to please her father who would no doubt prefer her wed.

And if she would wed no one, then, what else was possible but the convent? Once briefly, not so long past, it had even been her desire. Yet now, visibly with child, she could no longer presume to enter there.

Darkness lay upon and about her. No door was open to her.

Launcelot must, must come round, grow to love me, she thought. *By the force of my love he shall come to love me.*

I shall die, if he will not love me, I will go to him in death. She looked down into the well. Green moss clung to the cold, grey, descending stones. The water below was dark, and she could not make out how close or how far its surface was. *Like the maid of Astolat, on river barge I will go to him, for life is dark. The night is vast and the stars so far away. Holy mother, I drown. There is no earth more beneath my feet.*

Yet the stars need no earth to uphold them. The clarity of these words, coming like a gentle whisper from within, made her catch her breath.

Then why I? she asked. She lifted her head, brushed her hair back from her face with her hand, straightened tall. *Am I not earth enow for the seed within my womb? Launcelot loves me not? Then I shall do without the love of Launcelot. The cloister is closed to me? Then shall I do without the cloister.*

> *I love, and that suffices.*

> *I enclose the infant within my womb, and that is* *enough.*

> *My own life shall suffice.*

CHAPTER 24

Knowing her secret was no longer safe, she at last confided in Lady Breusen. To her utter surprise, Lady Breusen only said, "Ah, then we have some sewing to do."

Pelles also, when told, only nodded with both a smile and graveness upon his face, and said, "His destiny will be great."

"It was as if he knew," Elaine said in a puzzled tone to Pellehan later, as she sat by the river, he in his skiff by the bank. "He was not even surprised."

"And you were?"

Elaine started to answer, then stopped. "No," she said wonderingly. "No." She looked at the fisher with pondering eyes. Then, accusingly, "The messages—the queen's ring—it was a deception, was it not? Why? Why was it done?"

"That the prophecy might be fulfilled. It was a cursed arrow bearing only misfortune for all Britain—and in the end it shall be indeed its very destruction—which one day lodged its ill-fated passion for the queen in Launcelot's heart. One wonders whose malignant powers played its influence in that moment. Yet no matter. However great a curse, it cannot impede what is destined —though perhaps its consequences must cause destiny's fulfillment to pass along a more torturous route.

"But it was not the ring," added Pellehan. "The ring gave only the opening."

"That what happened might happen?"

"The ring opened up the space and the time. What was between you and Launcelot was already there."

Elaine's thoughts went back to the moment when she had paused with the grail before Launcelot that first evening.

"It was foretold in the prophecy," said Pellehan. "It was said you would bear Launcelot du Lac's son, and that the quest of the grail should be his."

As he spoke, the mist of a dream's memory emerged before Elaine: *the maiden of the western realm was to bear to the noblest of Arthur's knights the son whose quest would reach the grail...*

She had forgotten the dream. She had had no thought of sleeping with Launcelot; her intent had been only to bid him farewell, and to receive a farewell of him, some final words perhaps to treasure. She had certainly had no thought of conception, and only now understood the deception that had set the scene and the reason thereof. But now, sitting across from Pellehan, her present knowing penetrated back to that night. And to the morning preceding it, to the meal of fish shared at this very place. She realized there had been a knowing there, and a purpose, beyond and within and greater than Launcelot's passion, or her longing, or the deception which had brought them together in the bedchamber at the castle of Case.

A new sense of peace came to dwell within her as the months of pregnancy progressed. She sewed garments for the baby, passed long hours sitting by the river, watching the fisher king in his skiff, and the silver and gold fish flickering beneath the water, and the fuchsia water lilies opening to the sky's stillness.

She knew as if by instinct the child's name: Galahad.

Summer was in its fullness, the sun ripening the fruit and the grain. In the garden the pear hung heavy and full upon the limb.

Then came summer's waning, and the grape swelled full and purple upon the vine.

Unexplainably, darkness would flood over her at times, and with it a great heaviness, greater than that which weighed her body and slowed her step. It seemed at such times she had only strength enough to make it through to the child's birth, to bear him forth as the sea yields forth its treasure, and then to die.

I bequeath you my longing and my love, she whispered to the child within her. *I leave you the grail. Whatever its quest means, it is for you, little one, it is for you.*

The leaves turned golden in the warm misted autumn sun.

Wistfulness sat with Elaine. She felt such opacity within, a solidity and a bodily heaviness which seemed to bind her spirit, and no longer let it lift upward like the lark upon the wing.

The chalice form of the red-gold birch and elms reminded her that she would no longer bear the grail at the Christmas feast, for such was the privilege of the fairest maiden of the castle, and she was maiden no more. A longing would come upon her then, and a deep sadness. She rarely went into the grail chapel, where the cloth of samite draped the grail's form, hiding it from her gaze. The golden trees, instead, became chalices for her now, lifting her longing to the infinite blue of the fall sky.

It was only as the leaves fell, and the branches opened their bareness toward the snow clouds of winter, and the baby swelled her belly large and full, that she began to understand that her very body had itself become a chalice.

ELAINE OF CORBENIC

CHAPTER 25

The first snows began to fall.

The baby dropped low, and Elaine felt its feet kick against her.

The holiday festivities came and passed, white samite replacing the red in the grail chamber for the feast days. There was no procession of the grail in the hall that year, and Elaine herself was more often to be found in the quiet of her chambers or walking in her garden in the stillness of the evening, listening to the sounds of the celebrations from a distance, her attention turned to the movement within.

She rode to the sea one day. "A mad urge for a pregnant woman," Lady Breusen had said, trying to dissuade her to no avail. Elaine took the valley way, not the mountain path; she had sense enough for that at least.

It was toward the close of the season of epiphany. The winter sun was warm and the ground lightly dusted with snow. She was heavily clad, and when she reached the coast she let her furred hood drop back, the better to feel the salt wind upon her face and hear the waves, blue and silver in the winter light.

It was while she was there, regarding the sea from her horse, that she felt the first slow billowing of pain.

By nightfall the pains had set in with full force and she lay in her bed, face wet with sweat. Lady Breusen and the midwife were in attendance by her side. The waves of pain came one upon the other, cresting then receding. As her labor grew more intense, the waves began crashing together, the first only half-receding before the next waves broke over them, taking her breath away.

Lady Breusen bathed her face, wiping with a cool towel the drops that beaded her forehead like spray left from the waves. Hour passed into hour, and the night approached morning.

The pain came densely on her now, in savage contractions, searing—searing until she thought she could bear no more. And still it increased, burning yet deeper, at times imperceptibly subsiding only to again well up and swell over her. "Jesu!" she cried out, "I can bear no more!"

Through the delirium of her pain came the words of Launcelot, distant seeming in time and space, but as clear in her mind as when he spoke them that fateful morning by the stream: *Yield to the waves. Dive into or beneath them. Let their force carry you as the surf bears the swimmer...as lover yields to lover in darkness' passion, approach in trust destiny's kiss...*

For a moment she rallied, drawing strength from the words, surrendering to the contractions and breathing through them, but the waves' ruthless onslaught soon left her utterly spent. As they started finally to ebb, she began to wonder if it was into death's darkness that she was being invited to yield.

To die, never having known the secret of the grail...

Then it is for you little one, child of my pain and of his, to find it, she said silently, *to penetrate the secret of the grail, this chalice that caught the stream flowing from the pierced side, the wine which would have spilt to the sea, and offers it for drink to the deepest thirst of the heart's core.*

And our tears, she thought, near delirious with the long sleepless hours of labor's pain, *our tears are caught also in the cup's fullness, the sea salt of our tears and crimson drops of our pain mixed with the precious wine...and so the grail becomes ours, found in our lives, water mingling with the wine of its sacred mystery, there, in the piercing of our hearts.*

Outside a bird's chirping heralded the dawn, a single bird that had braved the winter. Elaine's awareness focused upon the sound, plunged itself into the bird's sweet song as if diving beneath the pain, opening beyond time into the clear notes of a bird's singing that spring morning nine months ago by the stream, a stranger's hand upon her...and to that morning on the ramparts, the sounds of the swallows flying from their nests, the sunrise sparkling on the river below where the fisher king sat in his skiff...and to the lark's song that last morning in the chamber at Case where the night before, strong warrior hands had gently touched her face.

"Mother of God!" The cry broke from her lips, the sudden bearing down of her body frightening her.

The sun's first rays entered the tall arched window

and cast a square of light on the stone wall opposite. And Elaine with great wonder reached down to touch the tiny foot of the infant emerging from her womb.

Galahad.

ELAINE OF CORBENIC

CHAPTER 26

She brought the child to the grail chapel within a day of his birth, before even the baptismal feast. She knelt before the grail, hidden under the cloth of white samite, and silently held her newborn son before it, as if in a wordless offering of one to the other.

She nursed the child herself, refusing the wet nurse who was sent to her, cradling the infant in her arms by her chamber's window as the quiet snow fell against the castle walls. Her milk came flowingly, and she came to know well the searing sweet feel of a small mouth at her breast.

The spring rains came, as she suckled the child, and the summer sun, and the fall winds. A babe's fevers came and went also, she herself bathing the small forehead with cool compresses. Once, fever took her also. Her forehead burned and her limbs felt on fire. She felt herself drifting deeper into the enveloping warm darkness, and it was only the cry of the infant hungry at her side that drew her back from the fever's precipice.

In the summer, she carried the babe in her arms along the stream, and laid him on her mantle among the bluets. He smiled at the little roundels of sunlight dancing through the tree branches, reached his hands out to grasp at the sunbeams among the grass and shadows. And in the autumn, he played happily with the falling golden birch leaves.

The very sky seemed to smile upon the child, and wind and boy to share equal delight of each other. The child soon began to crawl, and before he even could walk, he climbed. Whenever he could, wherever stone lay upon stone, the boy climbed.

It was when the child took his first steps, toward winter's end, that pain at Launcelot's absence came again into Elaine's heart.

The boy reveled in the strength of his legs, laughing as he crossed the stone slabs of the hall from his mother's outstretched hand to the tapestry hangings on the wall, and as he ran into the midst of the pigeons in the courtyard lightly covered with snow, scattering them in a blinding white cloud. He would run up to the young squires and even the knights, and yelp with delight when they would grab him up and toss him into the air. But it saddened Elaine that his own father, the realm's greatest knight, was not there to see those first steps, not there to lift his son and take him proudly ahorse with him.

ELAINE OF CORBENIC

CHAPTER 27

It fell, not long afterward, that Sir Bors de Ganis, Launcelot's cousin, came to Corbenic. Pelles received him warmly, as did Elaine, her child on her lap. During their greetings Sir Bors' eyes kept returning to the boy.

"Surely..." he murmured, and looked up sharply at Elaine's face.

She nodded. "Yes, he is Launcelot's son."

A broad smile spread across Sir Bors' face. "He is very like him!" he exclaimed heartily, and reached out and tousled the child's hair. "May he prove as good a knight as his father!"

At the dinner afterwards, Sir Bors shared news of King Arthur's wars against King Claudas, an old enemy of the King of Benoic. Favor was on Arthur's side, and a final victory hoped for soon.

"And what news of the court?" asked Heloise.

Sir Bors proceeded with accounts of the most recent adventures of the knights of the round table, and of court alliances and intrigues. "Launcelot," he concluded, "has passed some long months imprisoned by Queen Morgana le Fey, and has only recently returned to court. I wit he'll be struck by the news of the child."

"Think you?" said Elaine. She had not sent word to Launcelot of the boy. If he had not loved her, she would not try to hold him by the child.

"Forsooth, he'd be a fool were he not," replied Sir Bors, who found the young mother the fairest woman he had ever seen.

Sir Bors' words called up long abandoned thoughts, forgotten hopes. Perchance if Launcelot had not been embroiled in whatever untoward adventure had been his with Morgana le Fey, he might have returned. Perhaps if they were to meet once more, the spark of love she swore had been present—and which could have grown within him during their separation—might flame into fullness.

Yet in truth he was not likely to come; despite the rekindling of her hope, she knew this. Then she must go to Caerleon. No help for her if she should pine year after year, scanning the horizon in patient hope for his return. She was not at the mercy of his fidelity or lack of it. By the holy virgin, did her love bear no power in itself? Was not the one who loved, loved back or no, truly lover? *Then by all the angels*, she thought, *shall I not go in the strength of my love to my beloved?*

Soon after Sir Bors' visit, King Arthur returned from France, his battles with King Claudas decisively won and his conquests secured. He sent out an invitation to all his subject as well as allied kings and princes to a great feast to be held at Whitsuntide in celebration of the victory.

When Elaine heard of the feast, she went to her father.

"Allow me, sire, to attend this banquet."

"It pleases me well that you should go to the feast. Go, array yourself as befits your rank. Spare no expense. Whatever you need you may have."

Lady Breusen, together with the keeper of the wardrobe and the clothiers, worked long hours in the week that followed, using the finest of fabrics, to prepare for Elaine attire for the royal feast, such that would do honor to her and to Lystenois.

On the morning of her departure she went down to

the river. "Wish me godspeed," she said to Pellehan.

The old fisher shook his head. "Do not go," he said. "You cannot force fate."

Elaine had not looked for his discouragement, nor did she receive it in a friendly manner. "I *will* force fate," she answered firmly. "Do the seasons you spoke of so long ago have so short duration? I *will* force fate."

CHAPTER 28

And so, clad in a kirtle of deep rose beneath a surcoat of cloth of silver, and wearing a mantle the rich colors of the sea, the Princess Elaine traveled to Arthur's court at Caerleon-on-Usk, leaving the child Galahad in his nursemaid's safe care. With her went a large retinue, among them several ladies-in-waiting, twice as many knights, and the Lady Breusen as well.

King Arthur himself rode out to greet her, together with Sir Tristram, Sir Bleobris, Sir Gawain and other of his knights to accompany her to the castle, where she was received with courtesy and admiration by all in the court.

Never had such splendor been presented before Elaine's eyes. Her father's hall was nothing in comparison to the regal glory here, the elegance of lord and lady, and the brilliance of colors of silk and velvet, veil and gown.

Bright banners decorated with coats of arms hung from the great rafters, and the stone walls were covered with massive, richly woven tapestries of intricate design. More nobility commingled in the hall than she had thought to exist in the world. Yet regard discreetly about her as she might, Launcelot was not among them.

The hour for the festal high mass was rung, and the queen entered the hall. Fair, flaxen haired, of proud, regal bearing, her green eyes flashing, the sound of her voice like pearly laughter—*she is indeed fair beyond imagination, this Guinevere*, the fisher king's daughter thought.

At the queen's side was Launcelot.

"My lady, the daughter of our friend, King Pelles of Lystenoys, the princess Elaine," Arthur said, presenting Elaine to the queen, and then, addressing Elaine, "My queen Guinevere. Sir Launcelot, of course, is known to you from his visit to your father's court."

"Welcome, princess," said Guinevere, her smile sweet, but her voice cool. "A chamber has been prepared for you near mine."

Elaine paid little attention. Her eyes on Launcelot, she felt suddenly cold, as if it were winter rather than summer. He inclined his head in greeting, but she might have been a stranger for all the acknowledgement in his eyes. Cold, colder than the mountainside valley stream, colder than the sea, and from a sinking depth as great, she faltered, "My lord Launcelot…"

"My lady?" he replied courteously—but Launcelot was renowned for his courtesy, was he not? "May your visit to court be an enjoyable one," he proffered when she said nothing more, and he turned away from her to follow the queen into the chapel.

During the long high mass which followed, a vertiginous sense of emptiness engulfed Elaine. Her eyes came to rest again and again on the queen. Yes, fair indeed she was. It was hardly to be wondered at that Launcelot's favor was upon her. What had she, Elaine, been to him but a child in a faraway valley, a brief moment in time past?

Yet repudiate it the morning after as you might, she thought defiantly, as all stood for the reading of the scripture, *you did lie with me. For that moment, you did choose me, and you did love me that night.*

The priest moved back to the altar for the offertory.

And I bore your son.

ELAINE OF CORBENIC

CHAPTER 29

Elaine did not see Launcelot again until the evening meal, where he sat at the queen's left. Elaine was seated beside Launcelot, to his other side. Sir Gawain was to Elaine's left, and, as was the custom, it was he who carved her meat and shared her goblet. It was Launcelot, she noted, who carved the queen's meat and shared her goblet. Arthur hosted a queen from the North Country at his right.

Gawain was kind, comfortable, handsome enough in his grizzled way, full of gallantries. Launcelot was wholly absorbed in serving the queen, and paid Elaine no glance; not once did his eyes meet hers. Swallowing came hard to Elaine, and she responded to Gawain's sallies as if from a distance.

"Right glad am I to have had the honor of meeting

you," Gawain said as the second course was carried to the table. "Word of your beauty has reached us from Sir Bors."

From Sir Bors, not Launcelot.

"No beauty such as the queen possesses," Elaine answered.

His eyes narrowed as he looked at her; then in a voice different from the tone of his pleasantries he said quietly, "Princess, Launcelot has been Guinevere's from the day she set foot in court—no one has been able to tempt him. That it even for one hour turned him toward you shows there must be enchantment indeed in your beauty, and great power."

Elaine lifted her head, looked at Gawain, her eyes acknowledging his words, yet with a slight shake to her head. Enchantment? Then she herself had been victim of it as well, she who had been happy in Corbenic's quiet valley, desiring no man to share her solitude. *Yet then, by God*, she thought rebelliously, *by right of whatever enchantment had linked the two together, did it not still bind them? Did enchantments fade so swiftly? Not so her love.*

Gawain offered her a slice of venison.

In the gallery above, the minstrels began their play.

As she bit into the piece proffered her, she felt a sudden clearness, as if the meat returned strength to her and the oppressive weight lying upon her since her arrival to Caerleon was being lifted and dispersed in the minstrels' melody. She reached forward, took the cup she shared with Gawain and drank from it, placed it back. Tilting her head, she relaxed back into her chair, regarding the assembly with alertness and sudden vivacity.

She turned toward Gawain, her back to Launcelot.

"Truly, never have I partaken of so sumptuous a feast," she said to him, "nor of such variety of game. At home, why it is fish more often than not." She took another sip of wine, and allowed her voice to became a bit louder. "Do you know, once the fisher sent a fish to our table this long," she said as she stretched out her hands to show its length, her right hand knocking against Launcelot's shoulder. "At times I also fished with him— when I was young and could escape my lessons."

You, too, ate fish with us, stranger to whom my shoulder is turned, she silently thought. *I come in no barge asking burial, nor your prayers. Corbenic's stream yields nourishment indeed, and whether you share meal with me again at its bank or no, I shall still swim in it— and would have rather my stream, in truth, than your court.*

The third course was brought forth, more roast meats and mince pies and sweet dishes. The princess Elaine talked merrily with Gawain. She laughed aloud at his jests and sallies, aimed at individuals in the court more often than not, and she dredged up incidents to match from her memory, describing them with zest, careless of her gesticulating arms.

It was impossible for the knight at her right to be unaware of her presence.

After the dishes were cleared away and a last cup poured out for all, entertainment began before the high table—a jongleur, then a minstrel, and finally a dancing bear.

Shadows drew long in the hall, and the torches were lit. Not long afterwards, the king rose to bring the evening to a close, for the tournament would begin early on the morn.

The queen rose in turn and motioned to Elaine. "My ladies will provide you with whatever you have need," she said. To Arthur likewise she bade goodnight. To Launcelot she said nothing, but Elaine saw her eyes signal a distinct message.

ELAINE OF CORBENIC

CHAPTER 30

The chamber prepared for the princess lay next the queen's, just before it in the passageway. The room was not large but, with all its fine furnishings, was more elegant than any room of their own castles of Corbenic or Case.

"I was a fool to have come," Elaine said to Lady Breusen as the latter combed out her hair. "A fool."

Lady Breusen said nothing.

"I do not know what I hoped for." She stood up abruptly. "Was that other night indeed a lie, indeed an enchantment? God, for me it had been better it had never been. He is so cold. It is that which I cannot bear; it is as if he despises me."

She pulled off her kirtle, strode in her chemise to the window and back again to the dressing table. "Will he sleep with *her* tonight?"

"I would wager, my lady, that she has placed you so close to her to ensure he would not come to you. And I would further wager she has already sent for him to bed with her, yes." Lady Breusen extinguished the candles, leaving one by Elaine's bedside.

"Would that I had not made such a fool of myself as to come! Lady Breusen, what shall I do?" Distraught, Elaine paced back to the arched window, looked out into the darkness.

"The morn is not yet come. The night is clear," Lady Breusen answered, pausing before entering the small antechamber where her own bed lay, "and there is more than one star to wish upon."

More than one star indeed. The sky scintillated with them, a myriad of silver fish swimming in the sky. Elaine stood by the window, listening to the quiet that lay upon the castle, the familiar stars and constellations bringing a balm to her spirits.

An hour, perhaps more, passed in unbroken silence, until a sudden restlessness moved her to the door. Opening it, she saw a figure approaching in the darkness. She stepped into the passage, blocking the way.

"Launcelot," she whispered.

"Sacré—Princess of Lystenoys, what do you want of me?" he whispered back coldly.

"To remember."

A long silence, the stone floor chill, the glimmer of flickering candlelight against the wall. After a pause, she added, "To ask about your son, and how he fares."

He said nothing for a long time, and she could not see his expression. Then gently he reached forward, took her face in his hands, cupped it upwards, looked at it a long moment, kissed her on the mouth. And then drew away.

"I remember," he said. "And there is a place in my heart where perhaps if there were no Guinevere in the world…"

"Launcelot…"

"But even if there were not, my little princess of the fish, we belong, you and I, to different realms. Leave me go, even as I must leave you be."

"I do not believe you have no desire but to pass me by to betake you to the queen's bed."

Another moment's silence.

"You speak true," replied Launcelot at last. "Your

presence casts a potent spell, one in which momentarily, yes, the queen's memory dims. But when morning comes, reason returns. And I will not offend her, nor will I hurt you. Leave me pass."

And he walked by her, down the passageway to the next chamber.

Elaine reentered her chamber. Leaving the door ajar, she listlessly crossed the room back to the window. The stars still watched from above. Quiet was in all the castle, save for muffled voices coming from next door within the queen's chamber.

There was the sound of steps and the voices became clearer. Launcelot must have paced to the window, followed by the queen. Their voices were now loud and audible.

"It was you I thought to find at Castle Case." Launcelot's voice was angry, taut. "I had word you awaited me. I expected you. I looked for you to be there. It was for you only that my desire was."

"Yet instead, you found her."

"I was deceived, as I told you. I drank a wine of enchantment that night, I swear."

"If it was truly an enchantment, why, my lord,

sorceresses can be burnt; are you ignorant of that? Would you bear the same testimony at a church trial? Or was it perhaps her serving lady who put the potion in your cup? Indeed, the Lady Breusen has a reputation for such skills. What a useful helpmate for a provincial whore seducing knights who come to her wasted land."

"Forbear maligning her, lady." His voice was low, hard. "If I fell under the night's deception, the fault was mine. She is wild, pure innocence."

"Waylaying you in the passageway—wild, pure innocence?" The queen's voice rose, mocking.

"Especially so, waylaying me there."

"Then go to her, my lord—go to her." The queen's voice was full of anger. It was matched by that of his response.

"By God, I will!"

ELAINE OF CORBENIC

CHAPTER 31

Elaine drew in her breath, drew in the stars watching, commended herself to them as footsteps sounded in the passageway, a whirlwind of confused emotion within her, and turned to face the doorway.

Launcelot entered, shut the door behind him, saw her form dark against the window. She did not move. He strode up to her, took her by the shoulders, drew her to himself without gentleness, the hardness of his anger in his kiss.

She reached her arms up, one hand brushing across his cheekbone to hold his head, delving into his hair, the other reaching behind his back, answering his kiss with the intensity of her own, drawing him close as if it were possible to merge two bodies into the same space.

The angry hardness of Launcelot lost its edge in the

closeness of her presence, yielded to desire.

Later, as she lay in his arms, both awake, she whispered to him, "He bears your name, Launcelot. He is called Galahad."

She awoke in the early dark hours of morning: at her side Launcelot was restless in his sleep, turning, tossing, muttering. More than once she made out the word "Guinevere," and the sound was as a knife in her side. *It is true then*, she thought, and let it sink in, *his love is for Guinevere*. She lay awake, and then as he tossed and again cried out the queen's name, she rose, cast a mantle over herself, went to the window. The night was beginning to lighten.

Abruptly the door flung open. It was Guinevere.

Elaine froze, heart pounding, silhouetted against the dawning sky.

"Princess!" Guinevere said in a tone of hard, cold fury. "You are banished from this court. Take your leave this morning and never dare come again to Caerleon." She pointed her ring-studded finger toward the door with regal authority. "Never."

"Guinevere!" cried Launcelot, waking. Confusion was on his face. "Where…? Were you not in my arms just now?" He looked about, puzzled, then his eyes rested on Elaine. With a groan, he sank his head back against the pillow, eyes closed. Then he reached over to the floor where his undertunic lay flung, and sitting, slipped it over his head, and rose from the bed.

"My lady," he said, "I swear in my dream I was with you, I swear it!"

"Traitor! Faithless lover!" the queen cried at him, hitting him upon the chest with her fists. "Deceitful champion!" Her eyes were swollen, red; it was clear she had been weeping.

He took hold of her hands. "Guinevere, I was drunk with anger last night in your chamber, I lost my head. I..."

Elaine looked on, wordless.

"So you slap me in the face with an insult, and flaunt it before all Caerleon that you have cast aside the queen for this young provincial arrival? Have I grown too old, am I too outworn for you?"

"You know that is not true. For love of God, though, hush your voice. For your name's honor, and for that of the king."

"Oh, so now I see: this young strumpet, this 'innocent' witch—she's less risk for you, isn't she? Far safer to fornicate with a provincial princess than to commit adultery with Arthur's queen, is that it?"

Launcelot drew a sharp breath. "Madam, I beg you..."

"Or will you swear before me, here, now, to bear witness against your sweet before the church's court, that her serving lady indeed laid an enchantment upon you?"

"Lady, leave her be. Let your anger fall upon me, to whom it belongs."

"Turn to her, Launcelot," the queen persisted still, her voice growing hard, implacable. "Turn to her and tell her an enchantment was laid over you, and you lay with her, then and now, without love, without one instant's weight of love."

Launcelot looked from one to the other: Elaine, pale, silent, her eyes dark fathomless pools; Guinevere, flaxen hair wildly strewn about, shouting, her green eyes fiery in her fury. He did not speak, and Elaine grew suddenly afraid for him, for the wild darkness of pain in his eyes was like a tidal wave.

It was the queen who finally broke the silence, whispering, "Begone."

Launcelot seized her by the shoulders. "Guinevere,

listen to me. Until I die, I am your knight."

She slapped him. "Begone, I said. Leave Caerleon. You have shown yourself as faithless to your queen as you are to your king."

A strange laugh broke from Launcelot.

"Leave?" he repeated, a crazed sound in his voice. "Yes. There is no way out but to leave. Farewell then, Arthur, my king, my lord, my brother: I shall wrong you no more. Farewell, Guinevere, my life, my love, my joy, my curse, for I cannot live without your favor. Farewell provincial princess, who would have fared far better had I never strayed into your province. Farewell also, Launcelot, cursed name—and cursed the day of my birth!"

Seizing his sword, he ran to the window, and leapt from it.

Guinevere screamed and ran to the window. The two women leaned over the casement and looked out. The early morning light showed Launcelot struggling through the thorn bushes that lay below the window.

"Thank God for the bushes below," breathed Elaine. "They have broken his fall."

"They are thorn bushes," said Guinevere. "They will

draw blood."

"What have you driven him to?" cried Elaine, turning to face Guinevere, anguish and fury in her voice.

"How can that matter to you? Begone, princess, if you are wise," the queen snapped. "If harm comes to him, I shall surely have you suffer for it, for he was the noblest knight of the king's court."

Below, clad only in his shirt, sword in hand, Launcelot ran across the still courtyard, through the gateway, and out of sight.

"You have surely driven him over the edge of madness," said Elaine sorrowfully, and she turned away.

"Get out, princess! Out!" the queen repeated loudly. "Where is your lady?"

The queen seemed ungovernable in her hatred. Elaine had the sense that had the queen a dagger that moment, she would have turned upon her with it. She answered, "Most like gone to see to the fetching of water."

"Then *I* will help you gather your things," the queen said, flinging open the chest by the bed. She seized the comb on the table and Elaine's gown of the day before, and threw them into the chest.

"No need, my lady. I do not need your help. I long to be away as much as you long to have me gone," Elaine said vehemently, looking about her at the disarrayed bed, the covers fallen to the floor, the open casement window.

ELAINE OF CORBENIC

CHAPTER 32

Accompanied through the forest by the king and several of his knights on her departure later that morning, Elaine confided in Sir Bors de Ganis all that had happened, for she trusted in his discretion, and she knew he was Launcelot's cousin.

"Fear not, my lady. I will speak with the queen," he said.

"Do what you might," Elaine said to him. "He is crazed by her disfavor, and I fear for him."

"I promise you, for I love my cousin well, I will not rest until I have seen him returned to court and peace restored between them," Sir Bors replied.

It was a bittersweet promise to the princess, though she was grateful for Sir Bors' words of assurance, and she rode on, her heart leaden within her.

ELAINE OF CORBENIC

CHAPTER 33

Elaine returned to Corbenic.

Though more than two years had passed between their encounters, she had never entirely eradicated hope, had never completely freed herself of the belief that one day Launcelot would come to her, that one day her love would hold him. She was forced, now, to realize that this was not to be.

He had not, mercifully, forsworn her at the queen's demand; the memory of that moment of silence was as an island of sunlight in the darkness of her grief. Yet all too clear was the reality that, even if a certain sense of honor toward her had stayed his words, even if there was some vein of tenderness in him for her, beside his love for Guinevere it was as nothing.

It was Guinevere's favor he lived for, Guinevere's

disfavor that could drive him to despair. Whatever hopes or illusions she had held onto about her relationship with Launcelot could never more be held. He would never come and take her to wife, never be father to his child. His love was for Guinevere indeed, and Guinevere was beautiful. Moreover, God only knew where he wandered now, driven in despair by the queen's displeasure.

A dream, a heart's hope, dies hard, even one little articulated and long submerged, and during the days and weeks which followed her return, grief would swoop on Elaine, the wild weeping of mourning for hope died, for love revealed absent. She understood the grief that forbade food and drink, that plunges one toward death.

Had only I stayed at the abbey, she thought. *If only I had not returned that day, met Launcelot that morning.*

Once, in her troubledness, she slept and dreamed, and in her dream she wept in the abbey garden, and the abbess, smiling compassionately at her, said, "God waits in the wine of our lives, the blood-red wine of our pain as well as our joy," and when Elaine wept still, the abbess gently kissed her brow, saying, "Do you not know that even as water was once turned into wedding wine, so through the last blessing of the cup the wine of emptiness was made sacrament of love's mystery?"

Finally the tears dried, and she played with little Galahad with lightness again, feeling herself in some way older, calmer, with perhaps the stirrings of beginning wisdom.

Sometimes she would return to the empty chamber which had once held the grail, and sit in its sunlit stillness. She took the child with her at times; he played with his ball and blocks while she sat, thoughts blending into the beams of sunlight. Once, watching Galahad play, Elaine could not keep her thoughts from turning again to Launcelot. As if gathering all her fallen tears into the chalice of her prayer, pouring them out into space, she found herself whispering: "May the tears of my heart become stars in your sky, Launcelot, rainbows in your darkness, wherever it is you wander. And may my journey onwards, offered for you, be in some way a blessing unto you."

The grail itself now seemed hidden from her by more than cloth of samite, and she did not go into the restored chapel that was its present home. *It is left for you, my son*, she thought, *to find the grail's secret. Surely I have passed the quest on to you in your very blood.*

"And surely you inherit it no less from your father," she added aloud, for if ever Britain held a knight to whom the quest should have belonged, it was he.

Launcelot. And where was he now? Most likely reconciled with the queen. Sir Bors would have brought him back to court, the queen would have restored her favor to him as lovers do after a quarrel, and her favor have made all well. The image of Launcelot, half clad, running with his sword through the gateway, though, still seared Elaine's mind. *I loved you poorly, to have led you to such a plight,* she sighed ruefully, *and I pray to heaven that my grieving might lead me into a vaster love, more steady and true.*

Months passed, and the lord Bromwell approached her again. At court he was always kind with the child, was there to give him a toss or lift him to his horse. While it warmed Elaine's heart to see Galahad receive Bromwell's attention, it made her feel even more the lack of having a father for her son. Her joy in Galahad was utter, but as the boy grew, she felt even more strongly an element missing: knew that the joy of both mother and child would be more whole, more complete, if there were a man at her side.

Perhaps Bromwell sensed that she was weakening. They were together one afternoon, watching the child play with his animals of clay. Bromwell placed his hand on her shoulder, a hand strong and kindly.

Elaine shook her head. "No, my lord."

Not listening, he took her to him, hand behind her head, and kissed her as he had once two years before. For a moment she yielded to the warmth of his closeness, the passion of his lips, a sudden draught after so many long months. Then slowly she pulled herself away, repeating, "No. No, my lord."

"Elaine, I love you. I would give you happiness."

"My lord, I thank you. But my love is elsewhere. I cannot."

"My castle needs a lady. My bed wants your warmth. My land needs sons."

"I have already borne my son, Lord Bromwell."

Suddenly she realized the truth of what she had spoken. Even if Launcelot never returned, while her love lay with him, his son at her knee, she could share no other's bed. It did not matter if Launcelot returned or no. What had passed between them had passed between them, remained. She needed no endless nights.

ELAINE OF CORBENIC

CHAPTER 34

Heloise came to Elaine not long after, face radiant. "Castor has spoken to King Pelles for my hand." Castor was a squire soon approaching knighthood, and Heloise had long been in love with him. Heloise tangled the ties in Elaine's mantle in hopeless knots in her giddiness, and Elaine laughed gently at her.

The marriage would not take place until after Castor's knighting, and perhaps for not some years hence until he proved his valor in arms, but a betrothal ceremony was held that spring. Elaine helped Heloise with her attire that day, later stood by them in the chapel. She watched as the two young lovers before the altar made their betrothal vows and Castor tendered Heloise the ring that was his pledge of marriage. As the others left and the sounds of merriment began issuing from beyond the door, Elaine remained in the empty chapel, her silent gaze upon the small, still tabernacle flame.

When Heloise attended Elaine that evening, she held the candle close to her hand to show Elaine the ring on her finger. "It was beautiful, the ceremony, was it not?" she asked.

Elaine smiled gently at the dreamy-eyed maiden. "Indeed. Now go and take your rest. I will make shift for myself."

Galahad was beginning to walk sturdily now, and Elaine had been taking him with her to the river, and along the valley paths. That next afternoon, leaving Heloise to her reveries, she took him to the headlands overlooking the sea.

The vast expanse of sky and sea reaching together to infinity opened her heart and she breathed deeply, letting a deep calm wash through her. Beside her on the slope, Galahad played on the turf, rolling pebbles to fall over the cliffs to the sea below. In the distance off the coast a small lone whale sent its spume into the air, a tiny vertical fountain in the midst of the horizontal sea.

Her solitude hung gentle upon Elaine as she stood there, like a royal mantle upon her shoulders, a fine and soft mantle enfolding her, graceful upon her.

The whale slowly moved seaward, became lost to the eye's vision, and the sun began its slow descent into the sea, a great white-gold ball alone in a cloudless sky. Elaine called the child to her, and the two began their return to the valley.

By the time they reached Corbenic, twilight clouds had drifted across the sky, violet and purple in the sun's setting light, and a strange peace came over her. *It is possible*, she reflected, *that by drinking our destiny to the full, we find ourselves plunged into a mystery of love—in its filling of the cup, the dark purple spilling of our lives not lost, nothing lost.*

And slowly, one year passed into the next.

ELAINE OF CORBENIC

CHAPTER 35

The child Galahad played now freely with the other children in the courtyard, and delighted in following the squires about and watching their games. Elaine, looking for him one late January afternoon, went into the wintry courtyard and saw him at the fringe of a group of children.

One of the older pages was surrounded by the other children who were doubling in laughter at his antics. He had a bowl upon his head, and a wood sword backwards in his hand. With all sorts of wild expressions on his face, he was pretending to menace the other children with the sword handle, all the while stumbling over his own feet.

"Help! Don't break my arms!" cried one mocking youth.

"Fool of Corbyne! After me! After me!" cried

another.

"I'm a boar! I'm a boar!" yelled a third. The others laughed, snorting derisively in unison.

"What is this new game?" Elaine asked of one of the squires on the edge of the group.

"Oh, it's the fool he's pretending to be, the madman who stays in the little hut. He appeared one day not long ago, running through the town. Boys and dogs were chasing after him with turves and stones. He turned on them and threw those he could grab—some legs and arms broke, they say—then fled toward the castle. Some knights and squires rescued him. I haven't seen him myself, but they say he's as wild wood and crazed as ever a man could be. Killed a boar single-handed, they say, too."

Elaine watched the children a moment longer, an odd queasiness growing within that she could not place her finger on.

It was only later that evening as she put her child to bed that her thoughts alighted on the image of his father leaping from the window that Whitsuntide morning more than a year past. She had not thought on him much in the months past, and was startled at the sharpness of the pain the memory brought.

February's feast of Candlemas came. The air was mild and sweet—one of those late winter days that presage the coming of spring. Castor had been knighted in great ceremony by the king that morning, and in honor of the occasion Castor gave gifts and garments to the servants and to the poor, even to the fool in the hut. A great feast was held, and afterwards many went to take their rest. Elaine had gone with her maidens into the garden, to taste of the warmth of the winter sun. She sat on a stone bench, trellised bare vines behind her, eyes half-closed, hearing and not hearing the conversations of the others about her.

"Elaine, my lady." It was Heloise, come up to her. She spoke in a low tone, eyes urgent.

"What is it?"

"There is a man sleeping by the well, my lady."

Elaine's heart burnt, though she knew not why. She stood, placed her embroidery aside.

"His hair is wild, yet he is elegantly clad in scarlet, and, despite his dishevelment, oh, so comely."

"In scarlet? There was a scarlet garment among those that Castor—*Sir* Castor now—gave out, and he gave it to the fool," said one of Elaine's maidens standing nearby and overhearing them.

"Peace," said Elaine, then, "and say no word." Turning to Heloise, she said quietly, "Bring me where he is."

Elaine followed Heloise beyond the cherry trees, tiny leaf buds beginning to swell on their bare branches, and beyond the pear trees, to the low well. To the man lying in sleep by the well, clad in scarlet, hair wild.

She knew who it was before she reached him.

Launcelot.

It was he. Hair unkempt, tangled; beard matted, wild; face haggard, gaunt. Scarce recognizable. Hardly the strong, world-wise knight who had once come to the halls of Corbenic so many seasons before. The serpent dragon he had slain had come back to haunt him, it seemed, possessing him within its coils of madness.

Here no lance-bearing hero, no dragon-slayer, no grail-finder; it was a man, broken, human, who lay in fitful slumber by the stone well. Elaine smiled ruefully at the thought of her childish dreams when the fair, fearless, noble warrior had first come to Pointe Corbyne: that this would be the one who would deliver her from the wasteland of her father's country, who would vanquish the uncanniness which lurked in the valley's mists, who would bring light and order into the mysteries of her life.

Launcelot, fighting now only wild boars. A madman, fleeing the stones of young children. This the one whom she had hoped to see pursue fear from her land? He who had been the idol of the land's maidenhood, feared and respected by knight, baron and king alike, now the brunt and target of children's laughter.

Launcelot.

She knelt down, regarded him a long moment. The murmur and laughter of the maidens' conversation, punctuated with occasional sounds from the courtyard of children playing at war, formed a low background to the birdsong by the pear trees. The sounds stopped at the well: a circle of stillness surrounded the sleeping man, the kneeling woman, the well.

Slowly lowering her head to his, she laid a gentle kiss upon his forehead. No dragon-slayer more, nor the one who would bring the grail's healing to the land, perhaps. Yet still Launcelot. And she loved him still.

The voices and laughter of the maidens coming along the path gradually broke into her consciousness.

She stood, quickly returned along the path and round a hedge to meet them.

"Go inside," she said, shooing them out from the garden, and she strode toward the keep.

In her chamber she called for Lady Breusen, and told her the identity of the madman in the garden. "Go ask my father that I may have a private word with him."

The king received her in a small antechamber.

"Sire, Sir Launcelot lies asleep in the garden by the well, and he is mad. Grant me four of your most trusted men to bear him, and a chamber for his rest."

"Whatever is necessary, I grant to you," the king said, and he called to him four such men, ordering them to follow Elaine to the garden, with Lady Breusen accompanying them.

CHAPTER 36

In the garden, Lady Breusen drew a vial from her pouch and passed it to Elaine. "Give this to him to drink," she said. "It will be a calming influence on him. For he has lost his wits, and if rudely awakened..."

Elaine knelt down, held the vial to Launcelot's lips, poured in the amber liquid it contained. She pushed the dark locks from his forehead. His eyes flickered, stared at her a moment without recognition, closed again.

She stood and Lady Breusen signaled to the four bewildered men, swords drawn protectively at the princess' side. "Three of you: lift him gently, and do not awaken him," Lady Breusen instructed them, "and one of you go ahead to clear the way, so that we may pass unnoticed."

The sun was bright overhead now, the garden awash

and pale in its winter light. The contrast left them nearly blinded as they entered the dark stairway winding upwards where Lady Breusen led them. One of the men stumbled, and Launcelot woke. "Where do you bear me? No, let me free! Tormenters! Let me be!" He thrashed about, but the herbal sedative had thankfully taken effect, and the men were easily able to restrain him. In the struggle his head knocked against the stairwell wall, and he again lost consciousness.

When they reached the chamber to which Lady Breusen led them, where some planks and a mat had been placed to form a bed, Elaine addressed the escorts: "Lay him there, and go now. My thanks." The men left in discreet silence. Closing the door after them, she realized with a start that it was the old grail chamber.

A narrow shaft of sunlight fell across the unconscious man's face. Pain, struggle and weariness lay writ on it. "Leave me," Elaine bade also Lady Breusen. The latter let her hand rest a moment on her lady's shoulder, then stepped out, closing the door behind her.

Quietness lay like snow in the tower chamber. The knight before her lay motionless as death. Elaine stood before the window, her absent gaze momentarily caught in the circle of a falcon arcing the sun, then turned to look again upon the man she loved lying in the shadow of the room. Who she had once dreamed would find the grail secret and bring renewal to the land. *Instead,* she reflected sadly, as she came and knelt by his side, *it is he who must receive healing from the grail, its secret perhaps never to be found, forever hidden in its depths.*

At nightfall Lady Breusen came to the room with food and drink. A fever had come upon Launcelot, who was still without consciousness. "It is well," she said. "The fever will burn out his illness."

Elaine listened only barely, and leaving the tray of food in the room, Lady Breusen departed.

The evening star appeared through the window slit, the blue of the sky darkening fast about it. *Grail which once I bore before you,* Elaine murmured, *grail whose presence fills this chamber still, be healing for this man whom I love.*

For three days and three nights Launcelot lay in delirium, tossed and turned in restless dreaming. A heavy stillness hovered upon the dreamscape surrounding him, sliced through by a grosbeak's sharp intermittent call, the pauses between interwoven with distant strains of a lute's melody. The dream was always the same: The queen's back was turned to him. Then slowly the queen turned, smiled seductively through a smoky haze. He tried to reach out to her but upraised battleaxes dashing against sword and mace hid her face from sight, and blood swirled, and moans and cries and wailing filled the erstwhile stillness. Stone tumbled upon stone, till there was only a rubble of broken rocks and broken bones, torn flesh, and riverlets of blood swirling through chaos and darkness.

Through the darkness and massacre, as sight slowly returned to his eyes and sound to his ears, there came to him, in the midst of deafening clamor and dark spray of blood, the still, cool image of the grail maiden.

The morning of the fourth day Lady Breusen forcibly led Elaine to her own chamber and bed. "Sleep. You are pale, and will soon yourself be in need of healing. I will tend him."

The next morning when Lady Breusen came to Elaine's chamber, where exhausted, Elaine had slept near twenty-four hours, she said, "He awoke a moment last night. He spoke your name."

Elaine reached to the chair where her kirtle hung,

stepped out of the bed, and slipped the gown over her tunic all in one flowing movement. Splashing water on her face from the round bowl Lady Breusen had placed next to her, she said to her, "Go. Take your breakfast. I will tend him now."

Heart be still, it is only a muttering of his delirium, she bade herself. *His heart is Guinevere's, and I have no demands on it.* Still, there was trembling within her as she opened the tower room door, stood upon its threshold.

I did not ask you here. I did not trick you here, she whispered silently, fiercely. *I did not even desire you here. My heart let you go at Caerleon two years past when I truly saw how little yours desired me. Yet fate brings you once more to our castle and to this chamber. My will is not strong enough to refuse fate. Even less your words.*

And she entered.

ELAINE OF CORBENIC

CHAPTER 37

Sunlight filled the room. Launcelot turned his head toward her, his eyes clear. Gone was the glaze of madness. He saw her, knew her.

"My lady."

"Launcelot."

He braced himself to see her better, then lay back his head, exhausted by the effort. He closed his eyes and she thought he slept, but then he turned again toward her and spoke. "This night in my dreams, you came forward, the grail in your hands, and I looked upon the grail...and then I awoke."

Tears were wet upon Elaine's face.

"Yet for the love of Jesu, tell me how I came here."

"My lord," said Elaine, "when you came to our castle you had lost your reason, were as wild wood as man can be. You were not recognized and were kept as a fool, and given shelter."

A grimace of pain crossed Launcelot's face.

"Then one of my maids discovered you sleeping by the well and led me to you. I recognized you, so we brought you to this private chamber where the grail had been kept, and it's by the grail's power surely that your reason has been restored."

"God help me! How many know of my madness?"

"Only myself, Lady Breusen, and my father, King Pelles," Elaine replied.

"Then I pray you keep it secret. As it is, I am too deeply ashamed to ever return to my own country. Leave me, please."

Elaine was already at the door when he spoke once more, quietly.

"My lady…"

She paused on the threshold, turned to look back where he lay.

"I owe you thanks."

Elaine nodded ever so slightly in acknowledgment of his words, and went out the room.

Launcelot slowly recovered color and flesh. The

king's barber cut his hair, and he began to resemble again the Launcelot of before, save older, older by more than the years which had passed. Oft-times after the evening meal, Elaine sat with him, playing the lute and singing to him before, falling silent and becoming newly awkward and shy, escaping the room. *Foolish beating of my heart, there is no reason to beat so,* she told herself sternly. *A curse on the blessed day which brought this knight once more to Corbenic's castle. My heart was quiet, I thought I cared no longer. But it did not become stone.*

As more of his strength returned, Launcelot spent afternoons in the garden. Elaine would sit near him, hands caressing the early spring flowers. She loved him still, she realized, perhaps even more deeply than before. Yet a new reserve was upon her. She would not, as twice before, approach him nor expect, neither hope for, any gesture from him. She chided herself, though, on how boorish he must find her provincial awkwardness after Guinevere's eloquent tongue. And she chided herself that she should care, that all her hard-gained solidity should have again dissolved with his return. Casting about for speech and not wanting to remind him of the court she knew he must long for, she asked him of his youth, of

Benoic, of France.

She heard more about the years when he had been spirited away by the water nymphs, living in their magical, fluid aqua world. He limned for her images of long-lost childhood dreams, memories of light and shadow and feel which, save for that other brief sharing, he had long since forgotten or believed to even have once existed. In the arid blaze of the king's wars, and of the queen's passion, the mists of childhood had long since evaporated.

He shared with her also early memories long hidden in the dust beams of the past, when a little boy Galahad, now Launcelot, had played at his French mother Elayne's knees. He described his memories of her, then young, but as she listened Elaine saw her as she might be now had she lived still, time-wrinkled face, wise gray eyes. "Elle était, Elayne ma mère, très gentille, très..." He spoke in his childhood tongue when he spoke of those early years, where memory merged with sound and smell. "There was a plum tree in the courtyard, fragrant in the spring, its summer plums juicy and sweet. My father was mostly away...there were the wars with King Claudas..."

How strange, Elaine mused, *is time, and time's*

spiralings, as if life were a melody with the same motif repeated again and again at intervals, only the octave different. And now I am become three. Elayne the mother, Elaine the maid, Elaine the lover. Your life, Launcelot, is encircled in the name Elaine, and I, I no longer know where I begin and end.

Elayne of Benoic, Elaine of Corbenic, Elaine of Astolat. The one who birthed, the one embraced, the one who died. Maid longing, lover surrendering, mother nurturing—all three have taken their turn in my knowing of you. Astolat, Benoic, Corbenic—these names form the alphabet of the geography of your life...and the alphabet of the phases of my being. Three phases, like those of the moon, and the fourth is hidden in darkness. The fourth phase does not belong to you.

Astolat, Benoic, Corbenic. And then? And then? After the flowering, fruit bearing, golden leaves to wind surrendering, what then? The fourth phase is hidden from the eyes of man. The fourth phase lies hidden in stillness, hidden in the heart of timelessness.

ELAINE OF CORBENIC

CHAPTER 38

Once, as they were walking outside the castle walls, Launcelot, thinking upon his dream, asked her of the grail. "I would kneel before it, would let my eyes see this sacred relic."

"You saw it when first you came to Corbenic."

"And I remember its strange power. Where is the chapel in which it is held?"

Elaine shook her head. "The time will arrive when the grail will come before all those gathered at Arthur's table; in its hour, it will come, even as I bore it once before the table at which you sat."

"Surely the greatest cathedral in Christendom will be raised for its honor."

"It will pass before the table only, Launcelot, and feed the assembly, then depart whence it came."

"Then all Britain's knights shall ride in its search."

Elaine regarded the wild roses in the blossoming thickets by which they walked, more delicate in their simple five-petaled wildness than those carefully tended in the garden bed within the walls. Yet more hardy, she knew, the depth of their roots penetrating greater than the thicket's height.

"Why will they seek it, Launcelot? This day to come when all Britain's knights will search out Corbenic, seek the gold grail within its stone walls? What will they do when they find it?"

"They will seek it. Why ask? For glory and honor, perhaps devotion...and because what else is worth the quest?"

"No thing else. Launcelot, Launcelot, I know the quest's impulse in one's blood, the over-arcing impulse. But this world is one of paradox, and what is sought is paradox, and its finding is paradox."

She was silent for a while, then said, "One came once already to Corbenic, I was told, questing the grail, and won the vision of the grail, yet failed."

"How is that possible?"

"He quested, he beheld it in wonder, but he did not

ask the question, did not penetrate its meaning."

"And the question?"

"I do not know that the question is the same for everyone," answered Elaine after a pause. Her steps slowly came to stillness. "But I do not think its answer is a cathedral. He who originally drank from it appeared in glory in his life only once, Launcelot, and Peter's response—who no more than Percivale thought to ask the question—was to build a shrine upon the spot. He needed no shrine, nor cathedral, on that spot: he was on the road to Jerusalem and death.

"And when he did drink from the grail on the eve of his betrayal, its wine was so bitter that his prayer in the garden later that night was that it be taken away. But he accepted it in the end, and they say it is the same grail that then served to catch the blood and water from his lanced side, to spill out light into our darkness."

She leaned down, lifted a wild rose to her face, drew in its rich fragrance.

"The question?" Launcelot asked again.

"What it serves," she replied this time. Her thoughts lingered a moment on her misty memory of Pellehan telling her of Percivale, that young, innocent youth seeking the grail—who'd felt to her a brother in their shared quest when she had heard the story.

"And the answer?"

"Some questions can only be lived out," she responded. "What I intuit is only this: The grail serves the wine poured out, the heart's blood poured out, the heart's love. It serves life poured out. It needs no shrine of gold. Nor is it, in the end, to be sought in Corbenic's keep: it is there in the midst of the heart's longing, in the midst of pain and betrayal, in the midst of love."

"And that its meaning?"

"Surely its meaning is as many stranded as the threads of a weaving. What I spoke is only one thread of meaning, the thread that I know today, like one thread of the silver and gold threaded samite which enfolds it."

She paused again, cast her eyes over the slopes, the clouds cresting over the hills and arcing across the sky, then quietly added, "What is important perhaps is to ask the question. To let our lives be the question. And our lives to live out the answer. The grail is not something to be possessed, I grow to suspect, Launcelot, but something to be surrendered to."

Her conversation with Launcelot stayed in Elaine's

thoughts over the next days, came back to her as she untangled the threads of an embroidery or helped with her ladies' weaving, and in quiet moments when she was alone. It returned to her, also, as she began to spend time again with her son, who had been left much in his nursemaid's care during the long days of tending Launcelot. Watching him at play with his little wood sword, she wondered if he would ask the question that Percivale had not, and what would be the question asked, and lived out, in his own life.

Launcelot came upon Elaine in the garden one day as she was playing with Galahad. The two were tossing a ball back and forth; that is, Elaine rolled it to Galahad and Galahad threw it to her, or rather, threw it, and it landed wherever. She did not know Launcelot was present, until Galahad tossed the ball sideways. As she turned to retrieve it, she saw the ball roll into Launceot's hands. He rolled it back to the waiting child.

"I see your face in him," he said to her. "And I see my mother's face."

"Your mother's and your own," she answered him.

His face revealed dawning realization. "Don't interrupt your play," he said, and he stood there watching as the two continued their game with the ball.

In tossing the ball to Galahad, Elaine remembered Pellehan's words to her when she had asked him once if Launcelot would be the one to bring the grail's healing forth. He had spoken in images: "The sword for the one that shall heal the king requires both scabbard and girdle in order for it to reach to its destination. No, Launcelot's is not the sword," Pellehan had continued, still cryptically. "The scabbard, yes. But the girdle that will hold this scabbard, woven of woman, is equally necessary. Only with both can the sword be sheathed...the sword that shall belong to the child born of your union."

Presently the child's nursemaid came to take Galahad for his rest. "No," cried the child laughingly when he saw her, and he ran and hid behind Launcelot's legs.

Launcelot reached down and picked the child up, held him high, regarding him well.

"Launcelot," Elaine said to the child, who was looking wide-eyed at the man who held him. "His name is Launcelot. Laun-ce-lot."

"Lanc-lot."

Launcelot laughed. Then he turned questioning eyes

to Elaine.

"Galahad," she said.

"Galahad," he repeated softly. Memory slowly returned to him of her whispered words that night at Caerleon: *He bears your name.* "Well go, Galahad, my friend, and take your rest so that you might grow a strong and peerless knight."

So saying, he gave the child to the nursemaid.

When he and Elaine were alone, and she risen to her feet, he said in a voice between wonder and a question, "He is my son."

"Yes."

ELAINE OF CORBENIC

CHAPTER 39

Elaine was content that Launcelot should be there, though there might be nothing between them more. She was content to ride by him; to converse with him, at times deeply, at times in jest; content to see him, at last, lift his child to his knee, tousle his hair.

The yellow lemon grass of spring blanketed the slopes overlooking the stream where Launcelot and she walked one quiet afternoon. Elaine knelt to pick some. Launcelot sat, leaning back against a protruding rock. She could feel his eyes upon her as she brought a blade of lemon grass to her mouth and sucked upon its bitter sweetness. The sun lay gentle upon them, the only sound the quiet lapping of the water below.

"For you," said Elaine, rising and holding out a yellow flowered grass stalk to Launcelot. He took it, then taking hold of her hand, drew her down toward him. She sat by him then, and together they watched the dragonflies flit over the stream, the afternoon's quiet broken only by the soft sounds of the water lapping, like the gentle happiness within her, softly against the shore.

One morning not long after, Launcelot asked, "Has your father a place wherein I might dwell?" How could he return to the court at Caerleon, he who had shamed himself before everyone?

Memory of his last night there had now returned to him in full. He had heard how he'd run through the courtyard half-naked, and accounts of his madness as he'd wandered the countryside wild and crazed were certainly known by all. He had disgraced his king, and surely forever lost his queen's pleasure.

"You jest, my lord."

"I jest not. I am in disgrace in my own land: I can never return."

Elaine went that afternoon to the king with Sir Launcelot's request.

"We are well honored to have such a one as Sir Launcelot as our guest," Pelles replied. "Since it is his wish to live in these marches, he shall have the castle of

Bliant, and you shall abide with him there."

Grown accustomed to the strange unfoldings of events, and the odd and sudden turns of fate, not questioning the king further, without protest or query, Elaine simply nodded acknowledgment. She returned to Sir Launcelot and reported King Pelles' answer, all too keenly cognizant of the ephemerality of such turns of fate.

Aware also that in his request Launcelot had included no word of her, Elaine allowed herself no fantasies of long ago held dreams reaching at last fulfillment. Yet she could not keep from arising within her a peaceful glow of quiet happiness to know she should for yet awhile still be near to Launcelot.

So it came to pass that the following week, King Pelles escorted Sir Launcelot and Elaine to the castle of Bliant. With them rode Lady Breusen with the child in her care, and the knights and the ladies who were to serve them. After several hours' ride, the entourage paused on a small hill to view the castle of Bliant, built on an island in the middle of a large lake. It was only meet perhaps that the knight once abducted of water sprites and the daughter of a fisher king should be led to a castle that stood in a lake's center. It would be to them an island in time, sequestered from the outer world, far from Arthur's court, outside of past and future.

CHAPTER 40

When the last cup had been passed at the table in the great hall on the night of their arrival, a page led Launcelot and Elaine to the freshly prepared lord's chamber. The page bowed before Launcelot, clearly awed by him, then left them. Elaine stood at the doorway. Launcelot had asked of Pelles a dwelling place. She would not presume more.

Launcelot, who had strode in directly, was unbuckling his sword. Elaine watched him, hesitant, as she cast about in her mind how to gracefully take leave. Launcelot looked over to her. Laying the sword aside, he came to where she stood.

"My lord," she began.

Before she could say more, he had placed his hands on her shoulders. He drew her to him, kissed her slowly.

Twice before she had passed the night with Launcelot: only now did she know the gentle happiness of waking in his arms with the morning light. The weeks that followed were to Elaine as a dream long ago relinquished. There were even hours she sat, needle in hand, before a tapestry frame, content. A quiet joy dwelled within her as she watched Launcelot engage in mock battle with his young son or, other times, tell him stories of adventures undertaken by the knights of Arthur's court.

Launcelot, who gave the castle the name Ile de Joie, "Joyous Isle," would also in some part of him always carry the memory of this time.

But, as midsummer set in, he chafed.

At night he lay by dark-haired Elaine, and dreamed of the green-eyed queen. Hearing Guinevere's name murmured in Launcelot's sleep one night, Elaine felt a lurch within her heart, and a sinking.

"He will forget," Lady Breusen reassured her, "but a man does not forget a lifelong passion overnight."

He will not forget, Elaine knew. *This sojourn together is borrowed time, he will not stay. You will let him go, when the time comes, as a mother lets go her son.*

Yet something in her protested. Sons were made to go forth, but lovers, to come together.

Launcelot woke. It took him a moment to remember where he was: No, not the king's castle at Caerlon. Bliant, with Elaine at his side.

"Sweet, what is it?" he asked, feeling the wetness of her tears.

"Naught, naught," whispered back Elaine.

Launcelot turned to his side. Mysterious Elaine, with unexplained tears and quiet ways. Too mysterious, too quiet. Guinevere would have spoken plain, Guinevere with her flashing green eyes, bright in passion, fiery in anger. Nothing watery or elusive about Guinevere. Guinevere.

Foolish, traitor heart, do not clench so, Elaine chided herself the following afternoon as she sat at her embroidery. *If my lord Launcelot chooses to go hawking alone with his companions today, why should he not?* Yet, when it was toward the supper hour and time for Launcelot to return, she suddenly did not trust her composure to meet him and went instead to walk along the shore.

That evening in the hall, Launcelot sat with an

empty seat at his side, charming the ladies at the table. When Elaine did not return by dinner's end, he found himself irked; now he should have to go seek her, draw her back. Why must she slip away thus, wander alone along the water's edge? With Guinevere it would have been different: Guinevere, haughty Guinevere, would not have disappeared so. Guinevere would have sparred with him, wittily or angrily, at times coldly, even cruelly, but passionate and direct. No daughter of a fisher king, she. No erstwhile bearer of a grail. Guinevere was substantial, fiery: meet mettle for his warrior spirit.

The evening was warm. Elaine walked in the ankle-deep water rippling into the shore. The golden clarity preceding sundown cast its special light over the water. Here her heart opened, and peace returned. The golden reflections on the water brought the grail to her mind, and she felt, of a sudden, a deep longing for Corbenic.

When Launcelot came up to her from behind, she turned to face him, her eyes brilliant dark pools shimmering with light. There was a fearless openness in her face that unmanned him.

"My lady," he said, his earlier annoyance forgotten, and likewise all thoughts of the queen, as he kissed her hand.

How different she was from the child, beautiful and shy as a gossamer thread, who had once evoked his longing for mystery and innocence, he reflected as he watched her comb her hair that night. There was a fullness about her, a breadth, as if in the last four years she had widened into her strength. A quality almost of the sea.

In some way she had let him go.

She had reached a plentitude in herself. She was no longer asking his strength of him, his wisdom. No longer was she the fisheress of his heart, and he caught, unsuspecting, on the hook of the enchantment of her dreams.

Or had she herself been the fish—silvery, darting, elusive, swimming into his heart? Or the stream itself in which the fish swam, catching the play of sunlight and shadow, and at the same time, for the moment, a knight's heart?

Now, in her presence, it felt like a meeting place of stream and sea.

She looked up, saw him watching her, laid aside her comb.

He crossed the distance between them, reached out his hand to touch her face. No undertow pulling him; he was fully conscious of his desire. She had cut the line of her longing loose; and free, like the tide pulled by the moon, willingly drawn like the warrior in him to battle, so was he drawn to her. Drawn with his warrior's fearlessness. No stream's current catching him in its spray, but depth of sea drawing him to further depths.

Seaweed layered rock, crevices opening to still pools. And deeper yet, the tide's pull and the slow rhythm of the sea beneath, reflecting a light warmer than the sun's, tasting of a wine deeper than any at the king's table.

CHAPTER 41

Yet as the days passed, coldness would again slip into his words, a cutting edge to his voice, and a shortness and impatience show itself toward her. Then he would repent of his unkindness and be gentle once again with her.

There was longing in Launcelot for Britain. It was not simply—or even—Guinevere; he missed also the king's court and his fellow knights, the feel of a sword in his hand, the dust of battle. Quiet moments of evening would often find him gazing in the direction of Britain, and more than once his eyes were wet with yearning. He had a shield made for himself, all of sable, and in the center a silver device depicting an armed knight kneeling before a crowned queen.

As for Elaine, there was no shield for her nor armor

to ward off the sharp pang that lanced her when one day she glimpsed the sable shield. So it was that, for her, the Joyous Isle became tempered with pain, bittersweet.

What she did not understand, as the weeks passed, was the restlessness within her own self. It was a restlessness that came in the odd moment, even when things were well between Launcelot and her. Sometimes in an evening when she was at the window, watching the sliver of new moon setting in the deepening blue, and Launcelot coming to lay his hand on her shoulder—she, strangely reluctant to be pulled away from the twilight stillness. Or in the morning at times, when she would waken early, and watch Launcelot asleep there beside her, and not know truly what he had to do with her.

Or during a long supper in the hall in the late summer evening, the conversation on the day's hawking or the morrow's hunt, and through the high arched windows above, long rays of sunlight catching the dust motes in the air. Of a sudden, the noise and ceremony of the hall would become oppressive to her, and there would emerge a longing within her to be alone and apart.

One night as she slept, she dreamed. It was a dream she had had once before, just after the headlands walk when she had seen the whale, its spurt of ocean spray fountaining into the sky. In the dream it was a fountain of life blood, of love. It flowed from the heart of the grail bearer of many names, and one of the names was Percivale's sister. As it flowed, it filled a bowl from which healing poured out, bringing the gift of wholeness. And when the fountaining life had poured itself out, the emptied bowl was laid in a ship with a great white sail, and carried by the winds to burial in the land from whence it had come and to which it must return.

The strange dream intensified the restlessness within Elaine's soul, even as the moon pulls at the sea's depths. Though its images were indecipherable to her, they evoked memories of her glimpse of the whale off Corbenic's coast, as well as of the grail; it was as a voice from unknown depths, imperceptible to the senses, calling to her.

The tapestry needle gradually lost its allure, and Elaine began to feel a stranger to herself. A longing rose in her for another time and place, for something known and lost. Or not lost, but for a while eclipsed, and now re-emerging like a penumbra at the edges of daily life. Something was calling to her, lay unsatisfied in her, and she began to see that she would not find it on the Joyous Isle, that Launcelot alone could not contain her inner longing.

CHAPTER 42

It happened soon afterward there was a joust within three leagues of the Joyous Isle.

"My arm aches to carry again a lance," Launcelot said when he heard of it. He called to him a dwarf and bade him go to the jousting, and to cry out when the knights were ready to depart that there was a knight in the Castle of Bliant who would joust against any challenger, and that any who would put him to the worse would win a gerfalcon. The dwarf was not to give Launcelot's name, but only to call him Le Chevalier Mal Fet, "the knight who has trespassed."

A great number of knights came, drawn by the challenge. None were from Arthur's court, and none recognized who it was that called himself Le Chevalier Mal Fet. For three days Launcelot jousted against them, and he had the better of all. And at the three days' end, he made them all a great feast. His laughter was hearty and his color good, his step lively. He looked once more like the Launcelot of old.

Elaine quietly regarded him as he drank and made merry with the knights about him. He would return to Caerleon. She knew it within her. *I must be growing older*, she mused, *or wiser. I accept it now as I did not before. He belongs to the king, to adventure, to the court's excitement. To Guinevere, not to me. My world is not his.*

Nor was his world hers, she recognized wryly. Even were he to ask to come back with him to Arthur's court, she would belong nowhere there. She could little see herself living amongst the intrigue, gossip, spying and protocol of the royal court, with never a moment of privacy, solitude or freedom; her son made a page, and she one of the queen's ladies-in-waiting. Launcelot would be a rare guest to her chambers between absences of months, even years, away in battle or quest. And even then, would it be to her chambers that he would first return, or the queen's?

She had her life, and its fullness would suffice. Truth to tell, there was yearning in her for Corbenic. The

Joyous Isle was an island in her own life's flow as well as in Launcelot's, circumscribed, unlinked from time's daily passage. An interlude. The river which arced along Corbenic's keep flowed into the sea; the falls which fed its stream came from the hills. Life there was linked with the rhythm and flow of the cosmos, the grail in the keep at its heart.

She desired to bring Galahad back to Corbenic. It was at Corbenic where his early years should be passed. And she was needed there. Lady Breusen, who had returned to Corbenic some weeks prior, and bore the burden of the castle's charge in Elaine's absence, was growing old and tired easily. Nor was it only the daily needs of a castle household's overseeing that required her, but who was there to walk to the river to share time with the fisher king, and to keep vigil before the grail until its hour was come?

And might not that very vigil, and inward journey of deepening presence to its mystery, be in some way blessing to Launcelot in his own journey onward? And perhaps likewise to Galahad himself when the time would come for him to go forth?

The great white sail of her dream came to her mind.

Her heart gently opened at the thought of returning to Corbenic. And she knew that ultimately it was not the castle's need which called her back, nor Galahad's, nor the impending loss of Launcelot: it was her own heart's need…and her heart's deep desire.

That night, as she lay with Launcelot, she realized the time was not far when she would sleep no more in his arms. *Aye, there will be a void,* she thought, *an oh-so-great emptiness that day when he leaves, all the emptiness of night fallen. Yet from my empty bed I shall watch the stars, the emptiness of night filled with stars. Night, a grail of stars.*

CHAPTER 43

Four days later, two knights were sighted from the north tower. A boat was sent to carry them across the water, and waited while the two conferred with each other. "Abide here, until I know what manner of knight he is," said one to the other. "It were shame unto us, as he is but one knight, that we should both do battle with him." The other agreed, and stayed behind on the far shore while the first knight crossed over to the island. Arriving at the castle gate, he bade the porter go to the lord of the castle and tell him there was come a knight errant to joust with him.

Launcelot armed himself, and soon the two knights faced each other on their chargers, lances lowered. The shock of their first encounter was so great that both horses and knights fell to the earth. They took out their swords and fought lustily like two boars, each receiving wounds but never slackening. At last, after they had fought two hours, his combatant asked Launcelot his name for he had never met, he said, such a knight.

"Le Chevalier Mal Fet," answered Launcelot. "Now, tell me your name."

"Sir Percivale de Galis," said the other.

Upon hearing his opponent's name, Launcelot threw down his shield and sword, crying, "What have I done to fight with you, one of Arthur's knights, once one of my fellows?"

"Whosoever you are, Sir Knight," ordered Percivale, raising his helm and scrutinizing the other with puzzlement, "tell me your true name."

"My name is Launcelot du Lac, the son of King Ban of Benoic."

"And to think I might have slain you, when I have sought you these two years!" cried out Percivale. He clasped Launcelot in a warm embrace, then added, "On the far shore awaits your half-brother, Sir Ector."

Sir Ector was quickly sent for, and the two brothers embraced, and neither man's eyes remained dry. Then much sharing took place, Percivale and Ector recounting the adventures of their two years of searching for Launcelot, and Launcelot relating what he could piece together of his own two years which had ended with him once again at Corbyne, and now lord of the island castle where they spoke.

The dinner that night in the great hall was a happy one for the three men. Elaine, however, found herself with little appetite.

"And now we have found you, will you return with us?" Ector asked, wiping a piece of grizzle from his beard with the back of his hand.

Elaine placed down her cup, waited for Launcelot's answer.

A shadow crossed Launcelot's face.

"I can never return. How could I face the shame? And why should I return? The queen has demanded my exile."

"That may have been so," said Ector, "but the queen, as likewise Arthur and all his knights, has been greatly in grief over your disappearance. It was from her coffers that the search for you was paid, more than twenty thousand pound. Return with us. There will never be a knight given more welcome a return."

The look of incredulity and unexpected relief that spread across Launcelot's face was clear to be seen. "Is it true, what you say?" he asked, his voice sounding almost angry.

Ector swore to what he had said.

"And so will you come back with us?" he asked again.

Elaine saw the brief flicker of blinding elation pass over Launcelot's face, followed by pain, struggle, then quiet, all in a moment's space.

"No," he said, turning his gaze away. "No, I will not return."

Elaine stared at him.

"But why?" Ector demanded. "You must return. For your king. For your queen. For all of us, your fellows of the round table. You are missed, Launcelot. You are sorely missed."

"There is time yet to decide," said Percivale calmly. "Our wounds have healing to do, Launcelot, yours as much as mine I dare say. No need to decide on the future this moment."

Launcelot stood, held out his hand to Elaine. "My lady."

Then, turning to his guests, "I bid you good night, my lords and dear friends."

He will leave, she thought, as she took Launcelot's hand and walked with him from the hall, though she was deeply moved by his words of refusal.

He is ready. He will go. And I am ready for him to go. As the leaves turn and fall in the autumn, he will leave, and I will see him no more. My quest is not his. I leave him finally to Guinevere. And I, I will return to Corbenic.

He will come again one day, in that time to pass he will come. But I will not see him then. Now finally is the ending. I let you go, she said to him silently, *in peace I let you go.*

For her, he was already gone. There was a heaviness in the bed chamber as they entered together. She could see struggle in his face, yet he said nothing, and was exceedingly tender to her.

My God, she thought, *is it possible he has so changed that some slender thread of love or duty now brakes his step, that for a moment's time he chooses me before Guinevere, and not in lightness? It is a moment I will treasure in memory more even than that of his coming.* But aloud all she said, as he sat down on their bed, was, "Go, Launcelot."

He stared up at her, emotion mixed on his face.

If he truly chose to stay—her heart caught, but something deeper than her heart said "No," and she knew, in however inarticulate a way, that whatever his decision, she needed within herself to return to Corbenic.

"Caerleon is in your blood. It is your home. Go."

He closed his eyes a moment, opened them, his face easier, and nodded. Then, regarding her, "My lady, will you also come?"

"No."

She had moved beyond his reach in some subtle way he could not put into words. She had given him freeness from her, and likewise, herself freeness. Knowing in some unspoken way that even did he desire to stay, that door was no longer open to him, Launcelot became conscious, perhaps truly for the first time, that Elaine had taken a place in his heart, had left in him a love and a longing, a peace and a loss that would never be attenuated.

Suddenly all was reversed. She was not losing him to Guinevere, he suddenly realized: he was losing her for

Guinevere. She had never vied for Guinevere's place in his life; she held her own place, and he had been invited into it for a moment's span.

"Elaine."

She lowered her eyes to his face, not in shyness now, but with a depth of knowing, like a deep cup filled with rich, dark wine, in whose reflection he could see his own self.

Launcelot reached out his hand, this time not in the assumption that what he desired was his without asking, but knowing himself the recipient. He caressed her face in a last and a first longing, as if to etch every curve and line upon his soul forever.

"I will come again some day, when the summons comes to Arthur's castle for the grail's quest."

"I will not see you then."

She realized in that moment the search for the grail would ever be a connection between them, despite the parting of their ways. Returning to court with Launcelot had held no allure for her, on that she'd been clear. It could be Guinevere were indeed a better support for Launcelot in his life than she could ever be. And that she stayed more connected to Launcelot in staying faithful to the grail's quest in her way, even as he returned to the king's service to do so in his, questing for justice and mercy in the king's lands.

The grail. Awake, later that night, she rose and went to the window. A grail of stars. *What of its mystery have I found,* she thought. *Only the mystery of our lives. Our lives to be drunk to the full, our destinies to be embraced, accepted...our lives poured out in love, offered, surrendered into the mystery. And in that, perhaps, found healing, and found the sacred secret of its wine.*

CHAPTER 44

The moment of leaving was awkward, as such moments so often are. Launcelot looked about his person, shook his head in disappointment. "I would fain have left something for my son. Alas, I have nothing, not even a toy sword of wood."

"He will have his own sword when the day comes," she said. Then, half in question, half in command, she said, "You will give him knighthood. When the time comes, you will give your son knighthood."

"Yes."

They stood without speaking. Percivale and Ector settled themselves into the boat waiting to ferry the three across the lake, where their horses stood on the far shore. Launcelot reached forward, kissed Elaine on the forehead, then turned and descended to the shore, without looking back.

Elaine turned likewise away.

She returned to the castle, climbed to the battlements. There, she watched the boat with the three knights cross the lake, watched it land on the far shore, watched them mount, watched the cloud of dust grow and then diminish in the distance under the blue sky.

I knew he would go. I accepted it, she thought, *even willed it. I have no demand on him. Why then is my face wet with tears?*

A sea gull soared on the wind over the trees. A sea gull far from the sea. The sea, the valley, Corbenic. *Corbenic awaits,* she thought. Her emptiness poured out, mingled with the emptiness of space, and the sea gull's soar filled her heart. A deep joy flooded her, and a deep peace. Into the wind she said, "Corbenic, I come."

Epilogue

Galahad, when he came of age, was brought to the abbey of his aunt, where he was prepared for the future day of his knighthood.

When that day came, at the vigil of Whitsun with all the fellowship of the Round Table gathered for the great feast, a mysterious lady came to King Arthur's court and summoned Launcelot. He went with her, and she led him to an abbey he had never seen. There a comely youth of gentle strength and noble bearing was brought to him, and the old abbess requested Launcelot give the youth knighthood. And so, though he did not recognize him, on the morn of the feast day at the hour of prime, Launcelot made his son knight.

Then Galahad came to the Round Table, accompanied by an unknown ancient knight clothed all in white. The old knight led him to the Siege Perilous, the empty chair long held vacant for the knight who would one day find the Grail—and perilous to all else. All drew their breath to see Galahad take seat in it. In that moment, Launcelot knew who it was to whom he had given knighthood.

The king then led Galahad and all assembled to the river on which floated a stone with the sword that had belonged once to the knight Balin, and which could not be drawn save by the best knight of the world. All had thought it Launcelot's, but Launcelot had declined the challenge, saying it was not his to take. Galahad effortlessly drew the sword from the stone in the water, and placed it in the empty scabbard at his side.

That evening as the knights of the Round Table were gathered for supper, a vision of the grail, covered with white samite, appeared in the hall in a beam of light. As the grail passed through the hall, each man felt his own heart's desire fulfilled; then it departed, they knew not where. Then Sir Gawain rose and swore before all that he would depart the morrow in quest of the grail, and not return for a year and a day without seeing it more clearly, and all of the Round Table arose and made like vow. The king was deeply grieved, for he knew that many who departed would never return.

And that night when the grail came to the king's table Launcelot was among those who vowed themselves to its quest, already its desire nascent within him from the long ago words, and deep eyes, of its onetime bearer. The following morning after mass, Launcelot went to the queen's chamber to take his leave; with tears Guinevere berated him, crying out he was abandoning her for the grail's quest. Swearing fealty, yet unswayed by her pleas, Launcelot joined the departing knights. And as he mounted his horse and put on his helm, from within him emerged the memory of that dark-tressed bearer of the grail, bearer of his son—she who had been to him, in her own way, grail and cup. And who had accepted that a person's fate be twined with a destiny or a person, without choice having been asked in the matter, accepted it of her life, and accepted it, matter-of-factly in the end, of Launcelot's life.

Thus the knights of the Round Table rode forth in the quest of the grail. Many returned with no luck, and many perished in their wanderings. In his own wandering, Launcelot came to find himself one day in great straits, his horse slain. Not knowing what direction to take, he lay down to rest, and in the twilight between sleeping and waking, a voice bade him enter the first ship he would find. Arousing himself, he set forth and came to a strand, where he saw a ship before him without sail or oar. Entering onto the ship, he was overcome by a sweet fatigue and, lying down on the deck, at once fell into a deep sleep.

When he awoke, it was day. The ship he was on was far out of sight of land, and he saw, behind the single mast, a low couch, and on it the still, veiled body of a woman. Enveloped in an aura of peace and a sweetness of scent, she seemed one lying in the repose of sleep rather than of death. A letter in the folds of the veil near her hand revealed that its bearer had woven of her own hair the girdle for the sacred sword that from ancient time had waited Galahad's coming; and that, in the company of her brother Percivale and Galahad, she had given the bowl of her life blood for the healing of another, and for the averting of battle. Thus she had reached the end of her own life, and the ship was bearing her to her final home, beneath the altar of the grail in the land to which Percivale, Galahad and Bors would one day bring it.

Many days and nights passed as the ship silently glided over still waters. Then one night the ship came to shore again. A knight rode up on his horse and, alighting, taking only bridle and saddle, he boarded the ship. When the knight took off his helmet, Launcelot saw that it was Galahad, his son, and the two embraced each other with great joy. For a long while, as days passed into weeks, they journeyed together on the ship.

At last the ship touched to shore again, and a knight rode up with a white horse for Galahad to mount, and father and son made their parting. Launcelot stayed on the ship. Over the days and nights that followed, the ship was driven by the wind he knew not where. He slept little but kept vigil, his few fleeting sleep moments threaded through by dream images of the grail—and of its bearer, whose life had so briefly yet irrevocably entwined with his—and he prayed that he might be worthy to once more see the grail.

Finally one midnight, Launcelot found himself come to a castle, for the ship had found its way up a river that had flowed into the sea; and entering the castle, he found a chamber whose door was shut. Sensing the grail was within the chamber, he knelt before the door, and though a voice forbade him entrance, the door opened to reveal to his eyes, in a blinding brightness and covered in red samite, the vessel which once he had beheld in Elaine's hands.

He fell to the ground, and for days thereafter Launcelot lay like one dead. When he awoke, he asked where he was and learned the castle was Corbenic. It was Pelles himself who came to him, greeting him with warmth, and, when Launcelot asked of her, giving him the tidings that Elaine had peacefully died in her sleep that past Whitsun. Launcelot stayed four days, then returned to Arthur's court in Britain.

Galahad in turn came to Corbenic, together with Sir Bors and Percivale. Receiving full vision of the grail and its sacred mysteries, Galahad anointed and healed the maimed fisher king, and healing came at last to the land.

It was more than three years after the beginning of the quest that Sir Bors returned to Caerleon, telling how the grail had been found and taken to a land beyond the seas; and how at the year's end, Galahad had left the earth and in that same moment, the grail had been taken up, not to be seen on earth again.

Author's Note

The story of Elaine of Corbenic is drawn from the brief Malory account of the three encounters between Elaine and Launcelot: the night of conception; the visit to Arthur's court; and the finding of Launcelot by the well followed by their sojourn on Ile de Joie.

The story is based on and follows the twelfth-century legend. I place Arthur's court at Caerleon-on-Usk, following Geoffrey of Monmouth in his chronicle *Historia Regum Britanniae* ("History of the Kings of Britain") and Marie de France in her *Lais*. Launcelot's coat of arms is taken from a fourteenth-century French manuscript illustration.

There are many, widely differing sources of the Arthurian and grail legends, as well as many variants. In some, Pelles and Pellehan are brothers; in others, father and son; in still others, one person. Elaine is spoken of as the daughter of the Grail Keeper in Malory and in legend as the daughter of the Fisher King. In Malory's version, in one chapter Pelles is himself the maimed king; in another chapter, the two are separate.

In his voluminous book on the holy grail, Arthur Waite provides a detailed survey and analysis of the numerous grail manuscripts and sources, and includes many historic and legendary details. In the Celtic church, for instance, there were hereditary relic keepers, holding relics such as a venerable cup or book of gospels in a special shrine; the relics were said to wander about, to heal the sick, and to be protected from the eyes of unqualified persons. Actual chalices apparently were so uncommon in Arthurian days as to be almost unknown; an historic eleventh century document mentions, among other deeds of St. Columbia, that he provided the British churches with chalices. According to one grail manuscript legend, Arthur was led into the chapel for the grail and on his return was able to provide the form for eucharistic chalices; before that time wooden bowls were used.

The grail itself has been a timeless, archetypal symbol over the ages. In *At the Table of the Grail*, poets,

Jungians, scholars and others explore the grail as a paradigm for one's own personal inner journey, as well as the feminine symbolism of the grail. Jungian analyst Helen Luke, in writing about the Grail myth symbols of blood and water in her book *Old Age*, asks, "Could it be that mankind's fundamental prayer for meaning will bring to each man and woman the answer hidden in [these symbols] if only we are *there* with the empty cup of our lives to receive it—that is, attending to whatever the present moment may bring?"

And on a contemporary website called Chivalry Now, author Dean Jacques shares his understanding of the symbolism of the grail as a universal archetype, suggesting that "the story represents our own encounter with the mystery of life. Our understanding is veiled [when we first encounter it]...if we are fortunate, we... dedicate our lives to finding it again...from that point on, our experiences in life contribute to our quest," and concluding, "The final lesson of the grail is this: there is a grand mystery to life that calls for our awareness and participation, and therein lies our fulfillment of life."

Sources, influences and counterparts from non-Western traditions, such as those described in J. Weston's

From Ritual to Romance, contribute further dimensions to grail legend. There is, for instance, the Vedic story of Rishyancringa, the hermit whose marriage to the king's daughter breaks the spell of drought that holds the land wasted; and in the central myth of the *Rig Veda*, the god Indra pierces the serpent/dragon Vritra, releasing the heavenly streams from their captivity. Indra's act also sets free the cows, symbolic of richness and fertility, and releases the sun which had been held fast within the rock of the underworld night.

The fish, symbol of life and its origin, is also a central focus for Weston in the symbolism of the fisher king in the grail legend. In Chinese Buddhism, the goddess of compassion, K'uan Yin, is depicted on or holding a fish, and in the Han palace of Kun-Ming-Ch'ih there was a fish carved in jade to which prayers were offered in time of drought. The fish also was considered a potent factor in ensuring fruitfulness, its influence often being invoked in marriage ceremonies: newly-weds in India waded into the water to catch fish; Jews in Poland, and likewise the Greeks, had the custom of holding a fish feast at the conclusion of the marriage ceremony.

Many such symbolic aspects thread through the

opening pages of the story of Elaine of Corbenic. Malory, for instance, begins the account of Launcelot and Elaine with two episodes: the freeing of a fair lady from a scalding steam prison to which Morgana le Fey had bewitched her (he has Launcelot speak of her as "the fairest he had ever seen," the same words he uses later when he sees Elaine); and the slaying of a buried dragon-serpent. The proximity of these episodes in the account hints at their relatedness to one another and to the whole, similar to the interrelation of elements in a dream or symbols in a story. Accordingly, I have interpreted the lady to be Elaine, with the suffocation in steam as a metaphor for the fear that suffocates her life in the wake of her dream. The slaying of the dragon serpent, as hinted by the Vedic and other legendary correlations, was also incorporated.

In a similar dreamlike fashion, in addition to the ambiguity around Pelles and Pellehan mentioned earlier, other identities in the Arthurian legend, too, seem to intertwine and merge. The Maid of Astolat, the only other named lover of Launcelot besides Guinevere, oddly bears the same name Elaine, as does also Launcelot's own mother. Similarly, Galahad and Percivale each may appear as the Grail hero, depending on the version of the Grail legend. And Percivale's sister is sometimes identified with the grail bearer, whose role belongs in other versions to Elaine, so that the same harmonics of identity that occur between the two lovers of Launcelot occur between grail bearer maidens. This twinning of identities is reflected even in Elaine's parentage. Given the confusion of the identities of Pellehan and Pelles, Elaine joins in the tradition of ambiguous conception shared by Merlin, Arthur, Mordred and Galahad—all of whose births took place under mysterious or questionable circumstances.

In Malory's account, Launcelot lay with Elaine thinking all the while she was Guinevere, both times drugged by a potent potion of Lady Breusen's. It seems clear that while the more magical an enchantment Launcelot might claim, the more efficacious an excuse it might have been to the queen, any such enchantment in reality was due more likely to the close presence of the princess than to any potion or brew. Here again I have leaned toward a more metaphoric interpretation.

In general, this has been the overall direction taken in this rendition of Elaine's story: the taking of legend as one would take a dream, searching for the meaning of its symbols and anchoring those symbols in life.

ELAINE OF CORBENIC

Excerpts from the Original Text of Malory's <u>Le Morte d'Arthur</u>

The following excerpts of original text of the account of Elaine of Corbenic and Sir Launcelot's encounters in Book XI, Chapters I-VIII, and Book XII, Chapters I-X, of Sir Thomas Malory's *Le Morte d'Arthur* are from William Caxton's 1585 edition of Sir Thomas Malory's text as edited by Sir Edward Strachey (1868), and produced by Mike Lough and David Widger (1998) in a public domain version. The account of Galahad, Launcelot and the Grail in the Epilogue was adapted from Books XIII and XVI (not included here).

ELAINE OF CORBENIC

BOOK XI, CHAPTER I

How Sir Launcelot rode on his adventure, and how he holp a dolorous lady from her pain, and how that he fought with a dragon.

AFORE the time that Sir Galahad was gotten or born, there came in an hermit unto King Arthur upon Whitsunday, as the knights sat at the Table Round. And when the hermit saw the Siege Perilous, he asked the king and all the knights why that siege was void. Sir Arthur and all the knights answered: There shall never none sit in that siege but one, but if he be destroyed. Then said the hermit: Wot ye what is he? Nay, said Arthur and all the knights, we wot not who is he that shall sit therein. Then wot I, said the hermit, for he that shall sit there is unborn and ungotten, and this same year he shall be gotten that shall sit there in that Siege Perilous, and he shall win the Sangreal. When this hermit had made this mention he departed from the court of King Arthur.

And then after this feast Sir Launcelot rode on his adventure, till on a time by adventure he passed over the pont of Corbin; and there he saw the fairest tower that ever he saw, and there-under was a fair town full of people; and all the people, men and women, cried at once: Welcome, Sir Launcelot du Lake, the flower of all knighthood, for by thee all we shall be holpen out of danger. What mean ye, said Sir Launcelot, that ye cry so upon me? Ah, fair knight, said they all, here is within this tower a dolorous lady that hath been there in pains many winters and days, for ever she boileth in scalding water; and...said the people, we know well that it is Sir Launcelot that shall deliver her. Well, said Launcelot, then shew me what I shall do.

Then they brought Sir Launcelot into the tower; and when he came to the chamber thereas this lady was, the doors of iron unlocked and unbolted. And so Sir Launcelot went into the chamber that was as hot as any stew. And there Sir Launcelot took the fairest lady by the hand that ever he saw, and she was naked as a needle; and by enchantment Queen Morgan le Fay and the Queen of Northgalis had put her there in that pains, because she was called the fairest lady of that country; and there she had been five years, and never might she be delivered out of her great pains unto the time the best knight of the world had taken her by the hand. Then the people brought her clothes. And when she was arrayed, Sir Launcelot thought she was the fairest lady of the world, but if it were Queen Guenever.

Then...when they came there and gave thankings to God all the people...said: Sir knight, since ye have delivered this lady, ye shall deliver us from a serpent there is here in a tomb.

Then Sir Launcelot took his shield and said: Bring me thither, and what I may do unto the pleasure of God and you I will do. So when Sir Launcelot came thither he saw written upon the tomb letters of gold that said thus: Here shall come a leopard of king's blood, and he shall slay this serpent, and this leopard shall engender a lion in this foreign country, the which lion shall pass all other knights. So then Sir Launcelot lift up the tomb, and there came out an horrible and a fiendly dragon, spitting fire out of his mouth. Then Sir Launcelot drew his sword and fought with the dragon long, and at the last with great pain Sir Launcelot slew that dragon. Therewithal came King Pelles, the good and noble knight, and saluted Sir Launcelot, and he him again. Fair knight, said the king, what is your name? I require you of your knighthood tell me!

BOOK XI, CHAPTER II

How Sir Launcelot came to Pelles, and of the Sangreal, and of Elaine, King Pelles' daughter.

SIR, said Launcelot, wit you well my name is Sir Launcelot du Lake. And my name is, said the king, Pelles, king of the foreign country, and cousin nigh unto Joseph of Armathie. And then either of them made much of other, and so they went into the castle to take their repast. And anon there came in a dove at a window, and in her mouth there seemed a little censer of gold. And herewithal there was such a savour as all the spicery of the world had been there. And forthwithal there was upon the table all manner of meats and drinks that they could think upon. So came in a damosel passing fair and young, and she bare a vessel of gold betwixt her hands; and thereto the king kneeled devoutly, and said his prayers, and so did all that were there. O Jesu, said Sir Launcelot, what may this mean? This is, said the king, the richest thing that any man hath living. And when this thing goeth about, the Round Table shall be broken; and wit thou well, said the king, this is the holy Sangreal that ye have here seen. So the king and Sir Launcelot led their life the most part of that day. And fain would King Pelles have found the mean to have had Sir Launcelot to have lain by his daughter, fair Elaine. And for this intent: the king knew well that Sir Launcelot should get a child upon his daughter, the which should be named Sir Galahad the good knight, by whom all the foreign country should be brought out of danger, and by him the Holy Greal should be achieved.

Then came forth a lady that hight Dame Brisen, and she said unto the king: Sir, wit ye well Sir Launcelot loveth no lady in the world but all only Queen Guenever; and therefore work ye by counsel, and I shall make him to lie with your daughter, and he shall not wit but that he lieth with Queen Guenever. O fair lady, Dame Brisen, said the king, hope ye to bring this about? Sir, said she, upon pain of my life let me deal; for this Brisen was one of the greatest enchantresses that was at that time in the world living. Then anon by Dame Brisen's wit she made one to come to Sir Launcelot that he knew well. And this man brought him a ring from Queen Guenever like as it had come from her, and such one as she was wont for the most part to wear; and when Sir Launcelot saw that token wit ye well he was never so fain. Where is my lady? said Sir Launcelot. In the Castle of Case, said the messenger, but five mile hence. Then Sir Launcelot thought to be there the same might. And then this Brisen by the commandment of King Pelles let send Elaine to this castle with twenty-five knights unto the Castle of Case. Then Sir Launcelot against night rode unto that castle, and there anon he was received worshipfully with such people, to his seeming, as were about Queen Guenever secret.

So when Sir Launcelot was alighted, he asked where the queen was. So Dame Brisen said she was in her bed; and then the people were avoided, and Sir Launcelot was led unto his chamber. And then Dame Brisen brought Sir Launcelot a cup full of wine; and anon as he had drunken that wine he was so assotted and mad that he might make no delay, but withouten any let he went to bed; and he weened that maiden Elaine had been Queen Guenever. Wit you well that Sir Launcelot was glad, and so was that lady Elaine that she had gotten Sir Launcelot in her arms. For well she knew that same night should be gotten upon her Galahad that should prove the best knight of the world; and so they lay together until underne of the morn; and all the windows and holes of that chamber were stopped that no manner of day might be seen. And then Sir Launcelot remembered him, and he arose up and went to the window.

BOOK XI, CHAPTER III

How Sir Launcelot was displeased when he knew that he had lain by Dame Elaine, and how she was delivered of Galahad.

AND anon as he had unshut the window the enchantment was gone; then he knew himself that he had done amiss. Alas, he said, that I have lived so long; now I am shamed. So then he gat his sword in his hand and said: Thou traitress, what art thou that I have lain by all this night? Thou shalt die right here of my hands. Then this fair lady Elaine skipped out of her bed all naked, and kneeled down afore Sir Launcelot, and said: Fair courteous knight, come of king's blood, I require you have mercy upon me, and as thou art renowned the most noble knight of the world, slay me not, for I have in my womb him by thee that shall be the most noblest knight of the world. Ah, false traitress, said Sir Launcelot, why hast thou betrayed me? anon tell me what thou art. Sir, she said, I am Elaine, the daughter of King Pelles. Well, said Sir Launcelot, I will forgive you this deed; and therewith he took her up in his arms, and kissed her, for she was as fair a lady, and thereto lusty and young, and as wise, as any was that time living. So God me help, said Sir Launcelot, I may not wite this to you; but her that made this enchantment upon…And so Sir Launcelot arrayed him, and armed him, and took his leave mildly at that lady young Elaine, and so he departed. Then she said: My lord Sir Launcelot, Ibeseech you see me as soon as ye may, for I have obeyed me unto the prophecy that my father told me. And by his commandment to fulfil this prophecy I have given the greatest riches and the fairest flower that ever I had, and that is my maidenhood that I shall never have again; and therefore, gentle knight, owe me your good will.

And so Sir Launcelot arrayed him and was armed, and took his leave mildly at that young lady Elaine; and so he departed, and rode till he came to the Castle of Corbin, where her father was. And as fast as her time came she was delivered of a fair child, and they christened him Galahad; and wit ye well that child was well kept and well nourished, and he was named Galahad because Sir Launcelot was so named at the fountain stone; and after that the Lady of the Lake confirmed him Sir Launcelot du Lake.

Then after this lady was delivered and churched, there came a knight unto her, his name was Sir Bromel la Pleche, the which was a great lord; and he had loved that lady long, and he evermore desired her to wed her; and so by no mean she could put him off, till on a day she said to Sir Bromel: Wit thou well, sir knight, I will not love you, for my love is set upon the best knight of the world. Who is he? said Sir Bromel. Sir, she said, it is Sir Launcelot du Lake that I love and none other, and therefore woo me no longer...

ELAINE OF CORBENIC

Book XI, Chapter IV

How Sir Bors came to Dame Elaine and saw Galahad...

THEN as it fell by fortune and adventure, Sir Bors de Ganis...rode unto King Pelles, that was within Corbin...And when the king and Elaine his daughter wist that Sir Bors was nephew unto Sir Launcelot, they made him great cheer...And ever Sir Bors beheld that child in her arms, and ever him seemed it was passing like Sir Launcelot. Truly, said Elaine, wit ye well this child he gat upon me. Then Sir Bors wept for joy, and he prayed to God it might prove as good a knight as his father was...

ELAINE OF CORBENIC

BOOK XI, CHAPTER VI

How Sir Bors departed; and how Sir Launcelot was rebuked of Queen Guenever, and of his excuse.

AND on the morn King Pelles made great joy of Sir Bors; and then he departed and rode to Camelot, and there he found Sir Launcelot du Lake, and told him of the adventures that he had seen with King Pelles at Corbin.

So the noise sprang in Arthur's court that Launcelot had gotten a child upon Elaine, the daughter of King Pelles, wherefore Queen Guenever was wroth, and gave many rebukes to Sir Launcelot, and called him false knight. And then Sir Launcelot told the queen all, and how he was made to lie by her by enchantment in likeness of the queen. So the queen held Sir Launcelot excused. And as the book saith, King Arthur had been in France, and had made war upon the mighty King Claudas, and had won much of his lands. And when the king was come again he let cry a great feast, that all lords and ladies of all England should be there...

Book XI, Chapter VII

How Dame Elaine, Galahad's mother, came in great estate unto Camelot, and how Sir Launcelot behaved him there.

AND when Dame Elaine, the daughter of King Pelles, heard of this feast she went to her father and required him that he would give her leave to ride to that feast. The king answered: I will well ye go thither, but in any wise as ye love me and will have my blessing, that ye be well beseen in the richest wise; and look that ye spare not for no cost; ask and ye shall have all that you needeth. Then by the advice of Dame Brisen, her maiden, all thing was apparelled unto the purpose, that there was never no lady more richlier beseen. So she rode with twenty knights, and ten ladies, and gentlewomen, to the number of an hundred horses. And when she came to Camelot, King Arthur and Queen Guenever said, and all the knights, that Dame Elaine was the fairest and the best beseen lady that ever was seen in that court. And anon as King Arthur wist that she was come he met her and saluted her, and so did the most part of all the knights of the Round Table, both Sir Tristram, Sir Bleoberis, and Sir Gawaine, and many more that I will not rehearse. But when Sir Launcelot saw her he was so ashamed, and that because he drew his sword on the morn when he had lain by her, that he would not salute her nor speak to her; and yet Sir Launcelot thought she was the fairest woman that ever he saw in his life-days.

But when Dame Elaine saw Sir Launcelot that would not speak unto her she was so heavy that she weened her heart would have to-brast; for wit you well, out of measure she loved him. And then Elaine said unto her woman, Dame Brisen: the unkindness of Sir Launcelot slayeth me near. Ah, peace, madam, said Dame Brisen, I will undertake that this night he shall lie with you, an ye would hold you still. That were me liefer, said Dame Elaine, than all the gold that is above the earth. Let me deal, said Dame Brisen. So when

Elaine was brought unto Queen Guenever either made other good cheer by countenance, but nothing with hearts. But all men and women spake of the beauty of Dame Elaine, and of her great riches.

Then, at night, the queen commanded that Dame Elaine should sleep in a chamber nigh her chamber, and all under one roof; and so it was done as the queen commanded. Then the queen sent for Sir Launcelot and bade him come to her chamber that night: Or else I am sure, said the queen, that ye will go to your lady's bed, Dame Elaine, by whom ye gat Galahad. Ah, madam, said Sir Launcelot, never say ye so, for that I did was against my will. Then, said the queen, look that ye come to me when I send for you. Madam, said Launcelot, I shall not fail you, but I shall be ready at your commandment. This bargain was soon done and made between them, but Dame Brisen knew it by her crafts, and told it to her lady, Dame Elaine. Alas, said she, how shall I do? Let me deal, said Dame Brisen, for I shall bring him by the hand even to your bed, and he shall ween that I am Queen Guenever's messenger. Now well is me, said Dame Elaine, for all the world I love not so much as I do Sir Launcelot.

ELAINE OF CORBENIC

Book XI, Chapter VIII

How Dame Brisen by enchantment brought Sir Launcelot to Dame Elaine's bed, and how Queen Guenever rebuked him.

SO when time came that all folks were abed, Dame Brisen came to Sir Launcelot's bed's side and said: Sir Launcelot du Lake, sleep you? My lady, Queen Guenever, lieth and awaiteth upon you. O my fair lady, said Sir Launcelot, I am ready to go with you where ye will have me. So Sir Launcelot threw upon him a long gown, and his sword in his hand; and then Dame Brisen took him by the finger and led him to her lady's bed, Dame Elaine; and then she departed and left them in bed together. Wit you well the lady was glad, and so was Sir Launcelot, for he weened that he had had another in his arms.

Now leave we them kissing and clipping, as was kindly thing; and now speak we of Queen Guenever that sent one of her women unto Sir Launcelot's bed; and when she came there she found the bed cold, and he was away; so she came to the queen and told her all. Alas, said the queen, where is that false knight become? Then the queen was nigh out of her wit, and then she writhed and weltered as a mad woman, and might not sleep a four or five hours. Then Sir Launcelot had a condition that he used of custom, he would clatter in his sleep, and speak oft of his lady, Queen Guenever. So as Sir Launcelot had waked as long as it had pleased him, then by course of kind he slept, and Dame Elaine both. And in his sleep he talked and clattered as a jay, of the love that had been betwixt Queen Guenever and him. And so as he talked so loud the queen heard him thereas she lay in her chamber; and when she heard him so clatter she was nigh wood and out of her mind, and for anger and pain wist not what to do. And then she coughed so loud that Sir Launcelot awaked, and he knew her hemming. And then he knew well that he lay not by the queen; and therewith he leapt out of his bed as he had been a wood man, in his shirt, and the queen met him in the floor; and thus she said: False traitor knight that thou art, look thou never abide in my court, and avoid my chamber, and not so hardy, thou false traitor knight that thou art, that ever thou come in my sight. Alas, said Sir Launcelot; and therewith he took such an heartly sorrow at her words that he fell down to the floor in a swoon. And therewithal Queen Guenever departed. And when Sir Launcelot awoke of his swoon, he leapt out at a bay window into a garden, and there with thorns he was all to-scratched in his visage and his body; and so he ran forth he wist not whither, and was wild wood as ever was man; and so he ran two year, and never man might have grace to know him.

ELAINE OF CORBENIC

BOOK XI, CHAPTER IX

*How Dame Elaine was commanded by Queen Guenever
to avoid the court, and how Sir Launcelot became mad.*

NOW turn we unto Queen Guenever and to the fair
Lady Elaine, that when Dame Elaine heard the queen so
to rebuke Sir Launcelot, and also she saw how he
swooned, and how he leaped out at a bay window, then
she said unto Queen Guenever: Madam, ye are greatly
to blame for Sir Launcelot, for now have ye lost him,
for I saw and heard by his countenance that he is mad
for ever. Alas, madam, ye do great sin, and to yourself
great dishonour, for ye have a lord of your own, and
therefore it is your part to love him; for there is no
queen in this world hath such another king as ye have.
And, if ye were not, I might have the love of my lord
Sir Launcelot; and cause I have to love him for he had

my maidenhood, and by him I have borne a fair son, and his name is Galahad, and he shall be in his time the best knight of the world. Dame Elaine, said the queen, when it is daylight I charge you and command you to avoid my court; and for the love ye owe unto Sir Launcelot discover not his counsel, for an ye do, it will be his death. As for that, said Dame Elaine, I dare undertake he is marred for ever, and that have ye made; for ye, nor I, are like to rejoice him; for he made the most piteous groans when he leapt out at yonder bay window that ever I heard man make. Alas, said fair Elaine, and alas, said the Queen Guenever, for now I wot well we have lost him for ever.

So on the morn Dame Elaine took her leave to depart, and she would no longer abide. Then King Arthur brought her on her way with more than an hundred knights through a forest. And by the way she told Sir Bors de Ganis all how it betid that same night, and how Sir Launcelot leapt out at a window, araged out of his wit. Alas, said Sir Bors, where is my lord, Sir Launcelot, become? Sir, said Elaine, I wot ne'er. Alas, said Sir Bors, betwixt you both ye have destroyed that good knight. As for me, said Dame Elaine, I said never nor did never thing that should in any wise displease him, but with the rebuke that Queen Guenever gave him I saw him swoon to the earth; and when he awoke he took his sword in his hand, naked save his shirt, and leapt out at a window with the grisliest groan that ever I heard man make. Now farewell, Dame Elaine, said Sir Bors, and hold my lord Arthur with a tale as long as ye can, for I will turn again to Queen Guenever and give her a hete; and I require you, as ever ye will have my service, make good watch and espy if ever ye may see my lord Sir Launcelot. Truly, said fair Elaine, I shall do all that I may do, for as fain would I know and wit where he is become, as you, or any of his kin, or Queen Guenever; and cause great enough have I thereto as well as any other. And wit ye well, said fair Elaine to Sir Bors, I would lose my life for him rather than he should be hurt; but alas, I cast me never for to see him, and the chief causer of this is Dame Guenever. Madam, said Dame Brisen, the which had made the enchantment before betwixt Sir Launcelot and her, I pray you heartily, let Sir Bors depart, and hie him with all his might as fast as he may to seek Sir Launcelot, for I warn you he is clean out of his mind; and yet he shall be well holpen an but by miracle.

Then wept Dame Elaine, and so did Sir Bors de Ganis; and so they departed...

Book XII, Chapter I

How Sir Launcelot in his madness took a sword and fought with a knight...

AND now leave we of a while of Sir Ector and of Sir Percivale, and speak we of Sir Launcelot that suffered and endured many sharp showers, that ever ran wild wood from place to place, and lived by fruit and such as he might get, and drank water two year; and other clothing had he but little but his shirt and his breech. Thus as Sir Launcelot wandered here and there he came in a fair meadow where he found a pavilion; and there by, upon a tree, there hung a white shield, and two swords hung thereby, and two spears leaned there by a tree. And when Sir Launcelot saw the swords, anon he leapt to the one sword, and took it in his hand, and drew it out. And then he lashed at the shield, that all the meadow rang of the dints, that he gave such a noise as ten knights had foughten together…

BOOK XII, CHAPTER III

How Sir Launcelot fought against a boar and slew him, and how he was hurt, and brought unto an hermitage.

SO came Sir Launcelot and found [a] horse bounden till a tree, and a spear leaning against a tree, and a sword tied to the saddle bow; and then Sir Launcelot leapt into the saddle and gat that spear in his hand, and then he rode after [a great] boar; and then Sir Launcelot was ware where the boar set his arse to a tree fast by an hermitage. Then Sir Launcelot ran at the boar with his spear, and therewith the boar turned him nimbly, and rove out the lungs and the heart of the horse, so that Launcelot fell to the earth; and, or ever Sir Launcelot might get from the horse, the boar rove him on the brawn of the thigh up to the hough bone. And then Sir Launcelot was wroth, and up he gat upon his feet, and drew his sword, and he smote off the boar's head at one stroke. And therewithal came out the hermit, and saw him have such a wound. Then the hermit came to Sir Launcelot and bemoaned him, and would have had him home unto his hermitage; but...Sir Launcelot...was so wroth with his wound that he ran upon the hermit to have slain him, and the hermit ran away. And when Sir Launcelot might not overget him, he threw his sword after him, for Sir Launcelot might go no further for bleeding; then the hermit turned again, and asked Sir Launcelot how he was hurt. Fellow, said Sir Launcelot, this boar hath bitten me sore. Then come with me, said the hermit, and I shall heal you. Go thy way, said Sir Launcelot, and deal not with me.

Then the hermit ran his way, and there he met with a good knight with many men. Sir, said the hermit, here is fast by my place the goodliest man that ever I saw, and he is sore wounded with a boar, and yet he hath slain the boar. But well I wot, said the hermit, and he be not holpen, that goodly man shall die of that wound, and that were great pity. Then that knight at the desire of the hermit gat a cart, and in that cart that knight put the boar and Sir Launcelot, for Sir Launcelot was so feeble that they might right easily deal with him; and so Sir

Launcelot was brought unto the hermitage, and there the hermit healed him of his wound. But the hermit might not find Sir Launcelot's sustenance, and so he impaired and waxed feeble, both of his body and of his wit: for the default of his sustenance he waxed more wooder than he was aforehand.

And then upon a day Sir Launcelot ran his way into the forest; and by adventure he came to the city of Corbin, where Dame Elaine was, that bare Galahad, Sir Launcelot's son. And so when he was entered into the town he ran through the town to the castle; and then all the young men of that city ran after Sir Launcelot, and there they threw turves at him, and gave him many sad strokes. And ever as Sir Launcelot might overreach any of them, he threw them so that they would never come in his hands no more…and then came out knights and squires and rescued Sir Launcelot. And when they beheld him and looked upon his person, they thought they saw never so goodly a man…And then they ordained him clothes to his body, and straw underneath him, and a little house. And then every day they would throw him meat, and set him drink, but there was but few would bring him meat to his hands.

ELAINE OF CORBENIC

Book XII, Chapter IV

How Sir Launcelot was known by Dame Elaine, and was borne into a chamber and after healed by the Sangreal.

SO it befell that King Pelles had a nephew, his name was Castor; and so he desired of the king to be made knight, and so at the request of this Castor the king made him knight at the feast of Candlemas. And when Sir Castor was made knight, that same day he gave many gowns. And then Sir Castor sent for the fool— that was Sir Launcelot. And when he was come afore Sir Castor, he gave Sir Launcelot a robe of scarlet and all that longed unto him. And when Sir Launcelot was so arrayed like a knight, he was the seemliest man in all the court, and none so well made. So when he saw his time he went into the garden, and there Sir Launcelot laid him down by a well and slept. And so at-after noon

Dame Elaine and her maidens came into the garden to play them; and as they roamed up and down one of Dame Elaine's maidens espied where lay a goodly man by the well sleeping, and anon showed him to Dame Elaine. Peace, said Dame Elaine, and say no word: and then she brought Dame Elaine where he lay. And when that she beheld him, anon she fell in remembrance of him, and knew him verily for Sir Launcelot; and therewithal she fell a-weeping so heartily that she sank even to the earth; and when she had thus wept a great while, then she arose and called her maidens and said she was sick.

And so she yede out of the garden, and she went straight to her father, and there she took him apart by herself; and then she said: O father, now have I need of your help, and but if that ye help me farewell my good days for ever. What is that, daughter? said King Pelles. Sir, she said, thus is it: in your garden I went for to sport, and there, by the well, I found Sir Launcelot du Lake sleeping. I may not believe that, said King Pelles. Sir, she said, truly he is there, and meseemeth he should be distract out of his wit. Then hold you still, said the king, and let me deal. Then the king called to him such as he most trusted, a four persons, and Dame Elaine, his daughter. And when they came to the well and beheld Sir Launcelot, anon Dame Brisen knew him. Sir, said Dame Brisen, we must be wise how we deal with him, for this knight is out of his mind, and if we awake him rudely what he will do we all know not; but ye shall abide, and I shall throw such an enchantment upon him that he shall not awake within the space of an hour; and so she did.

Then within a little while after, the king commanded that all people should avoid, that none should be in that way thereas the king would come. And so when this was done, these four men and these ladies laid hand on Sir Launcelot, and so they bare him into a tower, and so into a chamber where was the holy vessel of the Sangreal, and by force Sir Launcelot was laid by that holy vessel; and there came an holy man and unhilled that vessel, and so by miracle and by virtue of that holy vessel Sir Launcelot was healed and recovered. And when that he was awaked he groaned and sighed, and complained greatly that he was passing sore.

ELAINE OF CORBENIC

Book XII, Chapter V

How Sir Launcelot, after that he was whole and had his mind, he was ashamed, and how that Elaine desired a castle for him.

AND when Sir Launcelot saw King Pelles and Elaine, he waxed ashamed and said thus: O Lord Jesu, how came I here? for God's sake, my lord, let me wit how I came here. Sir, said Dame Elaine, into this country ye came like a madman, clean out of your wit, and here have ye been kept as a fool; and no creature here knew what ye were, until by fortune a maiden of mine brought me unto you whereas ye lay sleeping by a well, and anon as I verily beheld you I knew you. And then I told my father, and so were ye brought afore this holy vessel, and by the virtue of it thus were ye healed. O Jesu, mercy, said Sir Launcelot; if this be sooth, how many there be that know of my woodness! So God me help, said Elaine, no more but my father, and I, and Dame Brisen. Now for Christ's love, said Sir Launcelot, keep it in counsel, and let no man know it in the world, for I am sore ashamed that I have been thus miscarried; for I am banished out of the country of Logris for ever, that is for to say the country of England.

And so Sir Launcelot lay more than a fortnight or ever that he might stir for soreness. And then upon a day he said unto Dame Elaine these words: Lady Elaine, for your sake I have had much travail, care, and anguish, it needeth not to rehearse it, ye know how. Notwithstanding I know well I have done foul to you when that I drew my sword to you, to have slain you, upon the morn when I had lain with you. And all was the cause, that ye and Dame Brisen made me for to lie by you maugre mine head; and as ye say, that night Galahad your son was begotten. That is truth, said Dame Elaine. Now will ye for my love, said Sir Launcelot, go unto your father and get me a place of him wherein I may dwell? for in the court of King Arthur may I never come. Sir, said Dame Elaine, I will live and die with you, and only for your sake; and if my life might not avail you and my death might avail you, wit you well I would die for your sake. And I will go to my father and I am sure there is nothing that I can desire of him but I shall have it. And where ye be, my lord Sir Launcelot, doubt ye not but I will be with you with all the service that I may do. So forthwithal she went to her father and said, Sir, my lord, Sir Launcelot, desireth to be here by you in some castle of yours. Well daughter, said the king, sith it is his desire to abide in these marches he shall be in the Castle of Bliant, and there shall ye be with him, and twenty of the fairest ladies that be in the country, and they shall all be of the great blood, and ye shall have ten knights with you; for, daughter, I will that ye wit we all be honoured by the blood of Sir Launcelot...

ELAINE OF CORBENIC

Book XII, Chapter VI

How Sir Launcelot came into the joyous Isle, and there he named himself Le Chevaler Mal Fet.

...AND then, after this, King Pelles with ten knights, and Dame Elaine, and twenty ladies, rode unto the Castle of Bliant that stood in an island beclosed in iron, with a fair water deep and large. And when they were there Sir Launcelot let call it Ile de Joie and there was he called none otherwise but Le Chevaler Mal Fet, the knight that hath trespassed. Then Sir Launcelot let make him a shield all of sable, and a queen crowned in the midst, all of silver, and a knight clean armed kneeling afore her. And every day once, for any mirths that all the ladies might make him, he would once every day look toward the realm of Logris, where King Arthur and Queen Guenever was. And then would he fall upon a weeping as his heart should to-brast.

So it fell that time Sir Launcelot heard of a jousting fast by his castle, within three leagues. Then he called unto him a dwarf, and he bade him go unto that jousting. And or ever the knights depart, look thou make there a cry, in hearing of all the knights, that there is one knight in the Joyous Isle, that is the Castle of Bliant, and say his name is Le Chevaler Mal Fet, that will joust against knights that will come. And who that putteth that knight to the worse shall have a fair maid and a gerfalcon.

Book XII, Chapter VII

Of a great tourneying in the Joyous Isle, and how Sir Pervivale and Sir Ector came thither, and Sir Percivale fought with him.

SO when this cry was made, unto Joyous Isle drew knights to the number of five hundred; and wit ye well there was never seen in Arthur's days one knight that did so much deeds of arms as Sir Launcelot did three days together; for as the book maketh truly mention, he had the better of all the five hundred knights, and there was not one slain of them. And after that Sir Launcelot made them all a great feast.

And in the meanwhile came Sir Percivale de Galis and Sir Ector de Maris under that castle that was called the Joyous Isle. And as they beheld that gay castle they would have gone to that castle, but they might not for the broad water, and bridge could they find none. Then they saw on the other side a lady with a sperhawk on her hand, and Sir Percivale called unto her, and asked that lady who was in that castle. Fair knights, she said, here within this castle is the fairest lady in this land, and her name is Elaine. Also we have in this castle the fairest knight and the mightiest man that is I dare say living, and he called himself Le Chevaler Mal Fet. How came he into these marches? said Sir Percivale. Truly, said the damosel, he came into this country like a mad man, with dogs and boys chasing him through the city of Corbin, and by the holy vessel of the Sangreal he was brought into his wit again; but he will not do battle with no knight, but by underne or by noon. And if ye list to come into the castle, said the lady, ye must ride unto the further side of the castle and there shall ye find a vessel that will bear you and your horse. Then they departed, and came unto the vessel.

And then Sir Percivale alighted, and said to Sir Ector de Maris: Ye shall abide me here until that I wit what manner a knight he is; for it were shame unto us, inasmuch as he is but one knight, an we should both do battle with him. Do ye as ye list, said Sir Ector, and here I shall abide you until that I hear of you.

Then passed Sir Percivale the water, and when he came to the castle gate he bade the porter: Go thou to the good knight within the castle, and tell him here is come an errant knight to joust with him. Sir, said the porter, ride ye within the castle, and there is a common place for jousting, that lords and ladies may behold you. So anon as Sir Launcelot had warning he was soon ready; and there Sir Percivale and Sir Launcelot encountered with such a might, and their spears were so rude, that both the horses and the knights fell to the earth. Then they avoided their horses, and flang out noble swords, and hewed away cantels of their shields, and hurtled together with their shields like two boars, and either wounded other passing sore. At the last Sir Percivale spake first when they had foughten there more than two hours. Fair knight, said Sir Percivale, I require thee tell me thy name, for I met never with such a knight. Sir, said Sir Launcelot, my name is Le Chevaler Mal Fet. Now tell me your name, said Sir Launcelot, I require you, gentle knight. Truly, said Sir Percivale, my name is Sir Percivale de Galis, that was brother unto the good knight, Sir Lamorak de Galis, and

King Pellinore was our father, and Sir Aglovale is my brother. Alas, said Sir Launcelot, what have I done to fight with you that art a knight of the Round Table, that sometime was your fellow?

Book XII, Chapter VIII

How each of them knew other, and of their great courtesy, and how his brother Sir Ector came unto him, and of their joy.

AND therewithal Sir Launcelot kneeled down upon his knees, and threw away his shield and his sword from him. When Sir Percivale saw him do so he marvelled what he meant. And then thus he said: Sir knight, whatsomever thou be, I require thee upon the high order of knighthood, tell me thy true name. Then he said: So God me help, my name is Sir Launcelot du Lake, King Ban's son of Benoy. Alas, said Sir Percivale, what have I done? I was sent by the queen for to seek you, and so I have sought you nigh this two year, and yonder is Sir Ector de Maris, your brother abideth me on the other side of the yonder water. Now for God's sake, said Sir Percivale, forgive me mine offences that I have here done. It is soon forgiven, said Sir Launcelot.

Then Sir Percivale sent for Sir Ector de Maris, and when Sir Launcelot had a sight of him, he ran unto him and took him in his arms; and then Sir Ector kneeled down, and either wept upon other, that all had pity to behold them. Then came Dame Elaine and she there made them great cheer as might lie in her power; and there she told Sir Ector and Sir Percivale how and in what manner Sir Launcelot came into that country, and how he was healed...

Book XII, Chapter IX

How Sir Bors and Sir Lionel came to King Brandegore, and how Sir Bors took his son Helin le Blank, and of Sir Launcelot.

NOW leave we Sir Launcelot in the Joyous Isle with the Lady Dame Elaine, and Sir Percivale and Sir Ector playing with them, and turn we to Sir Bors de Ganis and Sir Lionel, that had sought Sir Launcelot nigh by the space of two year, and never could they hear of him. And as they thus rode, by adventure they came to the house of Brandegore, and there Sir Bors was well known, for he had gotten a child upon the king's daughter fifteen year to-fore, and his name was Helin le Blank. And when Sir Bors saw that child it liked him passing well...And on the morn Sir Bors came afore King Brandegore and said: Here is my son Helin le

Blank, that as it is said he is my son; and sith it is so, I will that ye wit that I will have him with me unto the court of King Arthur...Sir Bors and Sir Lionel departed, and within a while they came to Camelot, where was King Arthur. And when King Arthur understood that Helin le Blank was Sir Bors' son, and nephew unto King Brandegore, then King Arthur let him make knight of the Round Table; and so he proved a good knight and an adventurous.

Now will we turn to our matter of Sir Launcelot. It befell upon a day Sir Ector and Sir Percivale came to Sir Launcelot and asked him what he would do, and whether he would go with them unto King Arthur or not. Nay, said Sir Launcelot, that may not be by no mean, for I was so entreated at the court that I cast me never to come there more. Sir, said Sir Ector, I am your brother, and ye are the man in the world that I love most; and if I understood that it were your disworship, ye may understand I would never counsel you thereto; but King Arthur and all his knights, and in especial Queen Guenever, made such dole and sorrow that it was marvel to hear and see. And ye must remember the great worship and renown that ye be of, how that ye have been more spoken of than any other knight that is now living; for there is none that beareth the name now but ye and Sir Tristram. Therefore brother, said Sir Ector, make you ready to ride to the court with us, and I dare say there was never knight better welcome to the court than ye; and I wot well and can make it good, said Sir Ector, it hath cost my lady, the queen, twenty thousand pound the seeking of you. Well brother, said Sir Launcelot, I will do after your counsel, and ride with you.

So then they took their horses and made them ready, and took their leave at King Pelles and at Dame Elaine. And when Sir Launcelot should depart Dame Elaine made great sorrow. My lord, Sir Launcelot, said Dame Elaine, at this same feast of Pentecost shall your son and mine, Galahad, be made knight, for he is fully now fifteen winter old. Do as ye list, said Sir Launcelot; God give him grace to prove a good knight. As for that, said Dame Elaine, I doubt not he shall prove the best man of his kin except one. Then shall he be a man good enough, said Sir Launcelot.

ELAINE OF CORBENIC

Book XII, Chapter X

How Sir Launcelot with Sir Percivale and Sir Ector came to the court, and of the great joy of him.

THEN they departed…

And when Sir Launcelot was come among them, the king and all the knights made great joy of him.

ELAINE OF CORBENIC

ABOUT THE AUTHOR

Tima Z. Newman has had an interest in medieval times since childhood, and draws on the poetry of legend, fairy tale, and myth in her writing and work. She is the author of *Lucid Waking: Using Dreamwork Principles to Transform Your Waking Life* (2010), and she is a psychotherapist and dream workshop leader. A native of Minnesota, she currently lives in the San Francisco Bay Area.

If you enjoyed *Elaine of Corbenic,* consider these other fine books from Savant Books and Publications:

Essay, Essay, Essay by Yasuo Kobachi
Aloha from Coffee Island by Walter Miyanari
Footprints, Smiles and Little White Lies by Daniel S. Janik
The Illustrated Middle Earth by Daniel S. Janik
Last and Final Harvest by Daniel S. Janik
A Whale's Tale by Daniel S. Janik
Tropic of California by R. Page Kaufman
Tropic of California (the companion music CD) by R. Page Kaufman
The Village Curtain by Tony Tame
Dare to Love in Oz by William Maltese
The Interzone by Tatsuyuki Kobayashi
Today I Am a Man by Larry Rodness
The Bahrain Conspiracy by Bentley Gates
Called Home by Gloria Schumann
Kanaka Blues by Mike Farris
First Breath edited by Z. M. Oliver
Poor Rich by Jean Blasiar
The Jumper Chronicles by W. C. Peever
William Maltese's Flicker by William Maltese
My Unborn Child by Orest Stocco
Last Song of the Whales by Four Arrows
Perilous Panacea by Ronald Klueh
Falling but Fulfilled by Zachary M. Oliver
Mythical Voyage by Robin Ymer
Hello, Norma Jean by Sue Dolleris
Richer by Jean Blasiar
Manifest Intent by Mike Farris
Charlie No Face by David B. Seaburn
Number One Bestseller by Brian Morley
My Two Wives and Three Husbands by S. Stanley Gordon
In Dire Straits by Jim Currie
Wretched Land by Mila Komarnisky
Chan Kim by Ilan Herman
Who's Killing All the Lawyers? by A. G. Hayes
Ammon's Horn by G. Amati

www.ingramcontent.com/pod-product-compliance
Lightning Source LLC
Chambersburg PA
CBHW070917260626
47162CB00007B/2698